Best Served Cold

TAWDRA KANDLE

Best Served Cold
Copyright © 2013 Tawdra Kandle

ISBN: 978-1-68230-253-8

Dedication

Mandie, Amanda, Liz, Olivia, Melissa, Lola, Christine,
Stephanie-
All of whom constantly challenge me to be better than I am,
and whose humor, encouragement and love
keep me moving forward.
I love you all.

# Prologue

The dorm room was dark. Someone jostled me, and I caught the shadowy image of my best friend Ava, grinning at me in encouragement. I rolled my eyes. Nothing was going according to my plan.

Throwing a surprise party for my boyfriend's birthday had seemed like a good idea a month ago. But standing there, twenty minutes after he was supposed to show up, with way too many people crowded into his room with me, I was beginning to think I'd made a mistake.

The door flew open and banged against the wall. From the corner of my eye, I saw a few people jump out of the way, and then everything seemed to happen at once, in both slow motion and at top speed.

Liam was silhouetted in the doorway, the fluorescent lights from the hallway bleeding into the darkness of his room. He stumbled and fell against the door jam, bracing his back there to catch his balance. He couldn't use his hands, because one arm was wrapped around the waist of the small blonde whose mouth was on his, and the other hand was down her shirt.

Someone in the room gasped. And then the guy I'd stationed by the light switch flipped it on, and a few people who didn't have a good view of the door shouted, "Surprise!"

Next to me, I heard Giff, Liam's roommate, groan. "Shit, Liam."

I thought I was rooted where I stood, but somehow my feet propelled me across the room. I pushed through the wall-to-wall bodies until I was standing near the door.

Liam raised his eyes and finally seemed to notice everyone else staring at him. The girl he was holding—and groping—giggled and hid her eyes against his chest.

"What is this?" The slur in his voice was pronounced, and I gritted my teeth.

"It's your birthday party, dumbass." Giff was at my elbow again. "Your *surprise* birthday party. Julia put the whole thing together. Remember Julia? Your girlfriend?"

"Julia." Liam drew out my name as he always did when he was teasing me. "Julia. God, what a girl. Going to all this trouble for your ex."

His eyes met mine, and there wasn't any confusion or guilt in them. No hint of the drunkenness I heard in his voice. There was only cunning and a knowing cruelty.

I couldn't breathe. My lungs had stopped working, and now my head began to spin. Giff grabbed me by the arm, and on my other side, suddenly my best friend Ava was there, her hand on my waist.

"Ex?" I managed to get the word out, despite the lack of oxygen. "Since when am I your *ex*?"

Liam grinned, but again, there was no humor there. "Did I forget to tell you I was breaking up with you? Well, hell. I knew I was missing something. Guess I thought you'd get the picture when I stopped answering your calls."

My mind scanned the last week. I'd been so preoccupied with putting this party together—a party that encompassed every room on this side of the hall. Giff and I had begged everyone to pitch in, let us use the space. I could see the corridor behind Liam was now filled with people who had ventured out to see what was going on.

But had he really stopped calling me? Wouldn't I have noticed? We were both busy with finals. Sometimes we went a few days without seeing each other. I remembered being relieved that I didn't have to keep the party a secret in person, so maybe it had been longer than usual...

"No, you didn't tell me." I whispered the words, hating the weakness they betrayed. "I think I would have remembered that. You know, the guy I've been dating for over ten months—breaking up with me."

Liam still had his hand tucked within the girl's shirt. I could see that she was beginning to realize what was going on. She bit her lip and kept her eyes on the floor.

"Ten months? Really? Well, that's gotta be some kind of record for me." He turned to look at his roommate. "Right, Giff? Have I ever kept a girl around that long?"

"You're an asshole, Liam." Giff swung me around so I didn't have to look at my boyfriend—correction, *ex*-boyfriend—and the mortified girl in his arms. "Ava, get her out of here."

She took me by the hand and pulled, stopping in front of Liam so abruptly that I ran into her back. I saw dark fury in her eyes just before she slapped his face.

"You fucking idiot. How dare you do this to my best friend?"

For the first time since he'd thrown open the door, something like regret flashed in Liam's expression. Or maybe it was simply shock that anyone had stood up to him.

Ava turned back to me. "Come on, Jules. Let's go home."

She put herself between the couple of the hour and me as we squeezed through the doorway. I heard Giff behind us, shouting.

"Go home, everyone. Take whatever food and drink you want, but get the hell out of here. Party's over."

Chapter One

"I didn't even like him."

I threw down the shirt I had just pulled from my suitcase and sank onto the edge of my bed. "I didn't like him that way. I thought he was jerk. I didn't want to go out with him. Remember? I said that. I had a crush on Mason Thomas. I wanted *him* to ask me out. Not Liam-freaking-Bailey."

Across the room, sitting at her desk, Ava lay down her pen. She was surrounded by piles of glossy textbooks we had just picked up from the campus bookstore, and her laptop was open to the syllabus for abnormal psych. Classes didn't start until Monday morning, but we always came back to campus a few days early to get settled.

As she turned in her chair, I had the sense that Ava was smothering a sigh.

"Yes. You told me that. You didn't like him. You told

me then, you told me right after the birthday party, you told me during finals. You told me the night you got so drunk, I was afraid I wouldn't get you home. You told me the days you couldn't get out of bed because you'd been crying all night."

"I'm driving you nuts, aren't I?"

She gave into the deep sigh and regarded me with that ever-patient Ava stare I'd come to know and love in the three years we'd been roommates.

"Of course not. I kind of hoped that maybe over winter break, you'd have time to process this a little, maybe start to move past it. But here we are, and you're telling me the same things you did a month ago."

I groaned and dropped back onto the bed. "I'm a loser. I'm a loser who can't keep a boyfriend, even one I didn't want in the first place."

"Sweetie." Ava sat next to me on the bed and took my hand. "Seriously. I know you have to go through all the stages of grieving this relationship, and you have the added issues of humiliation. But it's been six weeks. Maybe it's time to move on."

Having a roommate who was a psych major had its own particular charm. Not that I didn't appreciate her support, but getting analyzed all the time could be irritating. I bit my tongue and just barely kept from rolling my eyes.

"If I knew how to move on, don't you think I would? I'm telling you, Ave, my heart isn't broken." She smiled a little and shook her head at my use of her nickname. She always said I was the only person who could further shorten a three-letter name.

"I'm not really grieving." I went on, ignoring the

interruption. "I mean, I miss having a date on weekends and someone to meet me between classes for coffee and I definitely miss-" I patted the bed. "You know, this. But I don't think I miss *him*."

"Then why are you still talking about him? Not to be mean, but if you don't care about Liam, why can't you let it go?"

"I think it's what you said before. Humiliation. I thought people would stop talking about it by now, but I still hear whispers. 'There's the girl who was dating Liam Bailey and didn't know he had broken up with her.'" I mimed a look of shocked glee.

Ava nodded. "He hurt your pride. I get that."

"And why did he dump me? What did I do? What did I *not* do? I wasn't clingy. I gave him space. But I was supportive, too. I showed up at his track meets. I tried to be the perfect girlfriend. I went to dinner with his parents when they came to visit. My God, Ave, I slept with him. I didn't plan to, but I let him talk me into it." I rolled over and burrowed my face into the blankets.

"Jules." Ava lay down next to me and put her arm over my back. "Don't. You didn't do anything wrong. He's a prick. Maybe he hid it for a little while, but prick will always come out."

I peeked up over one arm. "Prick will always come out? Is that a new Ava-ism?"

"Maybe. Ava-isms are always accurate."

Pulling over a pillow, I flipped around to lie on my back again. "Jamie says I need something to take my mind off the whole thing." I grimaced, thinking about my visit home for Christmas and the advice my sisters had given me. "Pretty sure I was driving her, Jen and our parents crazy. They were glad to see me come back here."

Ava bit her lip and tilted her head. I recognized that expression, too. "Your sister might be on the right track. You need to change up your routine, try something new."

I shook my head. "I'm not ready to date yet. A new guy is the last thing I want."

"I'm not talking a guy. I'm talking, like, a hobby. Volunteering somewhere. The best way to take your mind off your problems is to do something for someone else. Or, I don't know, play an instrument, or take dance lessons."

"Dance lessons? I don't think so." I paused and turned my head to look at Ava. "I did have an idea, though. It's not exactly volunteering or being selfless."

"That's okay." She turned so she was sitting on her knees, looking down at me, her eyes bright. "That was just one option. What's your idea?"

I smiled. "Revenge."

"Are you sure this is what you want to do, Jules?"

We were huddled in the corner booth of Beans So Good, the shabby little coffee shop just off campus. It was quiet for a Thursday night, but then again, the spring semester was just barely underway. Taking into account the sudden cold snap that had hit Birch College as well as all of southern New Jersey, it wasn't surprising that most people wanted to stay at home.

But Beans was our home-away-from-dorm, as Ava said,

the place we went when we couldn't stand looking at the same four walls anymore. She swore their espresso had saved her grades second semester freshman year when she was carrying an eighteen-credit load. She held one in her hand now, a serious expression on her face as she looked over the rim at me.

I stabbed my straw into the iced mocha on the table. "I don't necessarily want to do it, but I think I need to."

"You know what they say about holding a grudge. Free rent in your head and all that."

"I'm not holding a grudge. I'm righting a wrong. Sort of."

"So doing this—whatever this is—will change Liam? Make him realize he's a jerk?" Ava set her drink down, centering it carefully in the middle of the cardboard coaster. "You're not trying to get him back, are you?"

"Definitely not." I shook my head. "I don't want him back. I want to move on. But at the same time, I want Liam to know how bad it feels like to be treated like that. I need him to know that he was wrong. "

She nodded. "Okay. I get it. But how do you see this playing out? "

"I'm not sure," I admitted. "I haven't gotten that far yet. If I thought showing up at party with another guy would do it, I would. But that would mean finding someone who'd be willing to go out with me. I wasn't exactly turning them away before Liam asked me out."

"Julia, don't be ridiculous. If you wanted a guy, you could have one. The only thing that keeps boys away from you is that don't-touch-me attitude you have. That's why Liam saw you as a challenge. He wanted you because..." Her voice trailed off, and she frowned.

"What's wrong?" I pushed back my cup.

"Nothing. I was just thinking. I might have an idea." Ava straightened up, shifting her legs out from beneath her on the bench seat. "We need a plan. I want to give it some thought. I mean, you're talking about more than just slashing his tires and keying his car, right?"

"Defile the Beemer?" I clutched my heart in mock horror. "As tempting as that sounds, yeah, it wouldn't do the job. Not the way I need it to."

Ava smiled. "Then don't make any plans for this weekend. You and I are going to have a down-and-dirty get-even planning session. I'll buy the ice cream."

Chapter Two

It snowed the next two days, complicating life for the students who were in the middle of moving back into dorms on Saturday. I took advantage of the rare downtime to snuggle back down under the covers and read for pleasure, something that wouldn't be happening much if at all once the semester got underway.

Ava was busy, helping everyone get settled again. She was out most of Friday and all day Saturday with meetings and moving in students. Her job as resident advisor was the sole reason we still lived in the dormitory rather than in one of the campus apartments. Her family couldn't afford to pay for her tuition, let alone for room and board; being RA meant free lodging for her and a reduced amount for me, since she was entitled to a single room and chose to live in a double with me.

My parents didn't hate me living with the freshman in Gibbons Hall, either; it cost half what the apartments did. They covered my tuition, but I knew it wasn't easy. I was happy to save them some money and still share a room with my best friend.

"Good God, save me from whiny-ass freshman girls!" Ava slammed the door behind her. "I thought second semester was supposed to be easier. But no. They're out there trying to switch roommates, complaining about everything and anything. Remind me why I do this?"

I pushed back my pillows and sat up in bed. "Because putting up with them pays the bills and keeps us in the luxury we've become used to having." I spread my hand around the room, taking in the painted-cinderblock walls, tile floor and utilitarian furniture. "Can you imagine taking us away from all this?"

"Try me." Ava dropped onto her bed. "I know I'm lucky to have this gig. It's only days like this when I just want to strangle them." She rolled onto her side. "Well, maybe not even all of them. Most of them are okay."

I stood up to put my book on the desk. "We were there once, right? Remember Kerri? I bet she wanted to strangle us sometimes, too."

"Maybe." Ava pinched the edge of her pillowcase between two fingers, rubbing it back and forth.

"What is it?" Sometimes my roommate was about as opaque as an open window. I could almost always tell when something was eating at her.

"We had a transfer over here from Liddleton."

I shrugged. "Okay. So?"

"It's Rachel Shaw."

For a moment, I was lost. I didn't know many freshmen outside the ones who lived on our floor. And then it hit me.

"Rachel. That's Liam's new--" I couldn't bring myself to say it.

Ava scooted up so that she mirrored my position on her own bed, hugging her knees. "I don't know what she is to him, but she's the girl from the birthday party."

I closed my eyes and let my head bang back into the wall. "Shit."

"I didn't recognize the name when it came over on the forms, but then I saw her. She's rooming with Miranda Dyer."

"Why did she transfer over here?"

Ava shrugged. "Not sure. But she put in for it in the middle of last semester. Her form was dated early November. So it was before...Liam."

"Maybe. Or maybe he was already doing her, and she thought it would be convenient for us both to be on the same floor."

"I guess, but I don't really think so. When she saw me, her face got red and she looked really embarrassed. Like she didn't want to be there any more than I wanted her there."

I sighed. "Yeah. Even that night, I had the feeling she got sucked into a situation she didn't really understand. No pun intended."

Ava threw one of her small accent pillows at me. "Nice, Jules."

I kicked down the covers and swung my legs over the side of the bed. "Whatever. As long as she stays out of my way, I won't bother her."

She raised an eyebrow. "She's not part of the revenge

plan?"

"Nope. Like I said, she was probably just collateral damage."

"Good. I was afraid it could get awkward." She drew a deep breath and then hopped out of bed. "Okay. I'm running out to grab supplies for tonight. Want to come with?"

I scrunched up my nose. "Really? You're going to trudge through the snow to the parking lot to go get ice cream?"

"Yep. We have a special guest joining us, and one of the conditions of said guest was a specific kind of ice cream. See what I do for you?"

"Special guest? Who's coming?"

Ava buttoned her coat and tugged a green knit cap over her dark hair. "It's a surprise. You trust me, right?"

I frowned up at her. "Mostly."

Laughing, she patted my head. "Don't worry so much. I'll be back in an hour. Get dressed, please."

I made a face behind her back as the door closed and then fell back across the bed. Maybe it was the snow or the gloomy gray skies, but my energy level was at an all-time low. I wasn't motivated to do anything but climb back under the covers and burrow.

But I knew Ava wouldn't have any of that. If I didn't change out of my pajamas by the time she returned, I'd have to put up with her nagging. Easier to just bite the bullet and do what she said now.

I opened the bottom drawer of my dresser and dug around for clean sweat pants. After all, she'd only said I had to be dressed; she didn't make looking good a condition. My favorite soft blue yoga pants were stuffed into the corner, and

I pulled them out along with an oversized white t-shirt.

A whiff of cologne hit my nose, and my throat tightened. I shook out the shirt. The words on the front read BIRCH COLLEGE TRACK AND FIELD, and I bit my lip, remembering.

"Hey, Bailey! Nice time on the four hundred meter!"

I had nearly reached Liam's side after the meet was over when the guy who had been next to me on the bleachers interrupted. My boyfriend turned his attention from me to grin at him.

"Thanks, dude. Appreciate you coming out."

I made a face behind the guy's back. It was part of Liam's upbringing, I knew, to play what he called the noblesse oblige card. He was always thanking people for coming to meets the same way I'd heard his father, Senator Bailey, speak to constituents who attended fund-raising dinners.

"No problem. You are the team, man. Everyone knows you're the best runner on Birch's track team."

I caught the gleam in Liam's eye before he shook his head. "Aw, thanks, but that isn't true. We've got a great bunch of guys. Everyone does an awesome job."

"Dude, no way." The guy's gaze never wavered, but now I detected a slight sway and the undeniable scent of alcohol from the cup in his hand. Damn, he was wasted. Really? At three o'clock in the afternoon?

I knew if I didn't break up this little love fest, we'd be standing here forever, as Liam stood around being self-deprecating and the fan boy sucked up. I stepped a little closer and smiled at Drunk Guy.

"Hi, I'm Julia. It was a good meet, wasn't it?" Lame,

yes, but this guy was too far gone to care.

"Heyyyy." He drew out the word as he lurched toward me, and too late I saw the contents of his plastic cup coming my way.

Liam ducked neatly to the right, avoiding the deluge by mere seconds, so I caught both the liquid and the guy who had just spilled it. He stopped his fall by grabbing my left breast, which along with the rest of me now smelled like a distillery.

"What the hell are you doing?" I wriggled away and sucked in my breath, pulling at the wet shirt. "Are you crazy?"

"Oh, God, I'm sorry." Drunk Guy peered into his cup as though surprised gravity and momentum had worked.

"Yeah, I bet you're sorry. You're going to be a lot sorrier when I drag your ass over to the coach and let him smell you."

"Julia." Liam grabbed my arm. "Come on. It was just an accident." He grinned at Drunk Guy, and the conspiratorial wink made me clench my teeth.

"Bullshit. What kind of loser comes to a track meet drunk? And did you happen to notice I'm soaked?" As if on cue, a chilly April breeze drifted over us and I shivered, goosebumps covering my arms.

Liam scowled and then called over to where a group of his teammates were milling around.

"Bran! Can you come here for a minute?"

The skinny redhead broke away from the crowd and trotted over. "What's up?"

Putting one arm around Drunk Guy, Liam steered him around. "Can you help my buddy here get back to his room *or whatever? His drink had a run-in with Julia."*

Bran glanced over at me and his eyes widened, making me all the more conscious that both my shirt and bra were basically invisible at the moment. I looked like first runner up at a spring break wet t-shirt contest.

Liam must have noticed that too, because he moved to stand between the rest of the world and me.

"Come here." He put his hand on the small of my back and guided me around the bleachers to the relative shelter of the equipment shed's overhang. Dropping the duffle bag that had been over his shoulder this whole time, he dug around and pulled out his clean white t-shirt.

He moved his hands to the bottom of my t-shirt and tugged it up. "Put up your arms," he murmured, and despite my annoyance and chill, I obeyed". He peeled it off me, trailing his fingers along my side so that I shivered all over again.

Liam dropped the sopping cloth into his bag and skimmed his fingertips around the bottom of my bra, letting his knuckles brush the underside of my breast.

"I don't have an extra one of these for you." He slid fingers beneath the band, lifting it away from my skin. I sucked in a breath, and the side of his mouth turned up in a smirk.

"Still pissed at me?" He leaned over and pulled me tight against the warmth of his body.

"Yes." But it was nearly a moan as his hands ranged over my back and slid down to my backside. He pushed me tighter so that I could feel evidence of his desire.

"Liam, we're outside...and everyone is right over there."

"I know. But you're standing here without a shirt on..."
I tried to wriggle away. "So give me that shirt."
He sighed and shook out the tee. "Hands up again."
"I think I can put on my own shirt, Liam."

"Maybe, but this isn't your own shirt. This is my own shirt that I planned to put on now, so I don't have to wear a sweaty one. Since I'm making a sacrifice, I think you can at least give me a little thrill."

I lifted my arms, and he dropped the shirt over my head, allowing his hands to graze my breasts again as he smoothed it down.

I shook my head, stepping back. "You're incorrigible."

Liam grinned and tapped my cheek. "Can't blame a guy for taking advantage of a promising situation." He zipped up the duffle, tossed it over one shoulder and offered me a hand. "Come on, let's get back to my room. I need a shower, and we've got dinner with my parents in a couple of hours."

As we headed for his car, I used my free hand to lift the neck of the t-shirt up to my nose and inhaled deeply. Even though it had been washed, I could still smell Liam there.

He caught me sniffing it and an odd look crossed his face. Before I could figure out what it was, he tugged me closer and kissed the top of my head.

A sound outside the door jerked me back to the present, still kneeling by the dresser, the shirt clutched in both hands. I looked down at it, frowning.

In the last six weeks, I'd thought about Liam almost non-stop. Most of those memories had been the bad ones. Letting in one that wasn't hurt.

I balled up the shirt again and shoved it back into the corner against the particle board. I dug out a long-sleeved green tee and kicked the drawer closed.

Chapter Three

By the time Ava burst through the door, laden with grocery bags and covered in melting snow, I had showered and dressed in my comfy relaxing clothes. My wet hair was in a single braid down my back, and I had even made my bed.

"Look at you, up and being productive." She dropped the bags in front of our mini-fridge and unwound the scarf from around her neck. "God, it's messy out there. Snow was just tapering out when I came in. Traffic was a mess. It snows every year. Do people forget between times how to drive in it?"

I opened up my closet and took out our supply of paper plates, plastic spoons and napkins. "Pretty much. Did you happen to get any real food, or do we still have to go to the dining hall?"

"What do you think? I'm not going out in that again, not even to walk across campus." She produced two frozen mini pizzas and several bags of chips from one of the bags. "Go toss these in the oven, and we're good to go."

Living in freshman dorms as juniors had its disadvantages, one of which was not having our own kitchen. The community kitchenette was right next to our room, providing at least a working oven and sink. I slid our pizzas into the hot oven and stood guard over them until the time signaled that they were ready.

Back in the room, Ava surreptitiously uncorked a bottle of red wine, I ripped open the chips, and we laid out our plaid tablecloth to have a dormitory picnic. The door was propped wide, since it was school policy that RA's have regular open door hours. Since Ava and I were both old enough to drink, there wasn't a problem with having wine in our room, but it also wasn't something we wanted to advertise to the impressionable freshman. We drank it red plastic cups and hid the bottle behind my desk.

I bit into the crust of my pizza and smiled. "This is really good. I was hungrier than I thought. Thanks for braving the elements to get us food."

Ava tipped back her plastic cup of wine. "You're very welcome. What good is a revenge planning party without some snacks?"

I swallowed and swiped a ridged potato chip across the bowl of onion dip. "So are you going to tell me about this special guest? I can't believe you told anyone what we're going to do."

She tilted her head. "I didn't exactly tell him. I just wanted some insight, and-"

"*Him?* You're bringing a guy into this? Ava, God! What are you thinking?"

She leaned toward me. "Calm down. I want to tell you my idea before he gets here."

"I'm listening." I leaned against the side of my bed.

"So you want Liam to know how you felt, right? That's your ultimate goal."

I considered. "Yes. And if he gets a little humiliation along the way, I wouldn't complain."

Ava nodded. "I understand that. I thought about a lot of possibilities. You know, Liam's got a high profile on campus, and even just in town, with his dad and the politics and all." She bit her lip. "I actually came up with some plans that had the potential to inflict real damage, but I didn't think you wanted to go that far."

I played with the crust on my paper plate and thought about the shirt stuffed in my drawer. "No, I don't want to hurt him. I mean, I know he's a jerk. But..." I squirmed a little and didn't meet Ava's eyes. "He's not all bad. We had some good times, too."

"Hey." She laid a hand on my knee. "You okay? Sure you want to do this?"

"I'm fine." I managed a smile. "I just want to get past him, and I think this is part of it. So tell me your plan."

She nodded, all business again. "I thought about what we were saying the other night, that Liam saw you as a challenge. Remember when he first asked you out? You were shocked."

"Yeah, because I didn't like him. I liked-"

Ava mock-glared at me. "I know, Jules. My point is that you kind of blew him off. He asked you to a party, and you wouldn't say yes. That drove him crazy, and it's why he kept asking you out. And even after you started dating him, you weren't like the other girls who act like he's a god."

I nodded. "Okay, I see that. But I spent the last month and a half ignoring him just like before, and I really don't think it caused him any angst."

"Right. So I was thinking about this, and I happened to run into Giff. He still feels terrible about the whole thing. We were in an RA meeting together, and then we grabbed some coffee."

"I miss Giff." I sniffled a little. Liam's roommate had definitely been a perk of our relationship. He talked reality shows, cute shoes and cuter guys with me when Ava wasn't around.

"He misses you, too. And..." She paused, either for dramatic effect or because she wasn't sure she should say the next words. "He thinks Liam misses you, too."

I took a moment to let that settle into my mind. "Hmmm."

"How do you feel about that?" Ava fell into her therapist posture sometimes without even knowing it.

"Not positive. But I'm pretty sure I don't care. A few weeks ago, it might have mattered. I don't want to go back, though. And maybe Giff just sees what he wants to see."

"Giff does like you, that's true. Which is why he probably he made the offer."

I dropped the crust onto my plate and folded the whole thing in half before I stood up and chucked it into the trash. "The offer?"

"Yep. He offered to help you get Liam back."

I stood still for a moment. "Really? And what did you

tell him?"

A small smile curved on the side of Ava's mouth. "I told him yes. I invited him over tonight for snacks and a planning session."

Blinking slowly, I sank back to the floor. "Ava, what exactly are we planning tonight?"

"According to Giff, we're getting you and Liam back together. But my plan is bigger. Go along with Giff. We'll work it out so Liam wants you again, and then..." She spread her hands out. "What comes next is up to you. But if Liam's at the point where all he wants is you, the power is in your hands."

I dropped my head back, resting on my mattress as I looked at the ceiling. "I don't know, Ave. I don't know if I can deal with it. I mean, first, the idea of putting myself out there for Liam to hurt again—I don't think I could handle it."

"You won't have to. Remember, challenge. Keeping you just out of Liam's grasp is the point."

"She's not wrong." Giff stood in the doorway, snowflakes on the shoulder of his navy blue pea coat and red plaid scarf. His blond hair was damp, but his smile never dimmed.

"Giff!" I jumped to my feet and hugged him. "It's so good to see you."

"I've missed you." He squeezed me briefly, and I breathed in his expensive cologne. Walking through a department store cosmetics department always made me think of Gifford. He smelled pricey.

Ava took his coat and hung it from a hook in our bathroom, so it could drip into the shower rather than on the tile in our bedroom.

"What have we got here?" He pulled off his boots and dropped to the floor, surveying the reminder of our picnic. "Have you broken out the good stuff yet?"

"How about some wine?" Ava dug out another plastic cup. "There's a bottle of sauvignon chilled in the fridge and some shiraz here." She lifted the bottle. "Or if you're feeling a little sassy, we have rummy gummy bears, too."

Giff laughed. "I should be all sophisticated and adult and choose wine, but the bears intrigue me. Bring 'em on."

Ava took out the glass bowl that contained our colorful treat—gummy bears swimming in rum--and spooned a generous portion in the plastic cup. Giff eyed them with a mixture of curiosity and skepticism.

He finally snagged one between his thumb and forefinger, examined it and popped it into his mouth.

Chewing with his eyes closed, he nodded.

"I get it. Okay, I am now all about the bears in rum." He tossed a few more back and then licked his fingers. "Sticky little buggers, though."

Ava handed him a napkin, and Giff smiled at me as he wiped his hands. "What Ava said when I so rudely interrupted is exactly on target. Stay away from Liam. Don't try to see him."

"Oh, believe me, I'm not." I slid a glance at my roommate. "That kind of pain I don't need."

"Good girl. If Liam gets even a hint that you're still hung up on him, he'll run in the other direction. Screwed up, I know, but that's our boy."

I bit my tongue. I wasn't still hung up on Liam, but if this was what Giff needed to believe so he would help us, I was willing to go along with it. Behind his back, Ava raised her eyebrows at me. I lifted my shoulder in the slightest of shrugs.

"Giff, it's really nice that you want to help, but are you sure? I mean, Liam's your best friend. You don't feel like you're...I don't know, betraying him a little?"

He craned his head back to knock the last few bears out of the cup. "Jules, sometimes people don't know what's good for them. You were good for Liam. He was the happiest I've ever seen him. I don't know what spooked him. He didn't tell me. After the party, he wouldn't talk about the whole situation. Just said he was ready to be free again."

I sighed and stretched out on the floor along the edge of the tablecloth. "I think I know what it was. I didn't at first, but then the more I thought about it--"

Ava faked a look of surprise. "You thought about this, Jules? Really? I never would have known."

"Shut up." I kicked at her foot. "So I spent a little time wondering what caused my boyfriend of nearly a year to suddenly break up with me. Sue me." I turned back to Giff. "About two weeks before the birthday party, the Senator and Mrs. Bailey came down to take us to dinner. You remember that? You went out with us, too."

"Sure." Giff rolled his eyes back, thinking about it. "We went to the fancy-ass Italian restaurant, and Liam's mom didn't like her meal."

"Right. So the Senator made a big deal that night about some event this spring. He's getting an award—the Senator, I mean—and Liam is supposed to be a presenter or whatever. And his dad talked to me about it, told me it was really important and he hoped I'd be there with Liam."

Giff frowned. "Okay?"

I hugged my knees to my chest as I swung up to lean against the bed again. "Don't you see? His father assumed I'd still be with Liam at that point. I saw a look on Liam's face—he was not happy."

Ava nodded. "The thrill of the chase was officially long over. Once his parents were thinking of you as a long-term girlfriend, he was scared shitless."

"I don't know about scared, but definitely freaked."

"Yeah, that would be classic Liam." Giff sighed.

I rolled my eyes. "Maybe, but it's also the most ridiculous thing I've ever heard. Seriously? So you're a guy, you have a girl who's hooking up with you on a regular basis, someone who as far as I can tell, you don't hate, and just because your parents approve, suddenly you turn asshole? And not only that, you feel the pressing need not only to break up with said girl, but do it in the most hurtful, dick way possible?" I shook my head. "I call bullshit."

"You're not wrong. But trust me, sweetheart, it's the truth." Giff lay down and reached an arm to the fridge, snagged the bottle of white and sat up again. He unscrewed the top and poured a healthy slug into the cup that had held the rummy bears.

"I've known Liam since the first day of high school. I was cocky, with a huge chip on my shoulder about being the scholarship kid at the prep school. And believe it or not, he was geeky and quiet. He was all about the running. We were lab partners in chem, and somehow, we hit it off. I've seen him change, saw what the whole 'I'm the Senator's son, chicks dig me' deal did to him."

"Yeah, I'm sure it was a horrible thing to go through, all that privilege and girls throwing themselves at him. However did he rise above it?" Ava didn't use sarcasm often, but money and position were sensitive subjects for her.

Giff cocked an eyebrow. "Hey, we all have crap to go through. I'm just saying that a lot of what you see with Liam came from all of the insecurity. Don't you ever wonder why he still lives in that tiny little dorm with me instead of getting an apartment? Believe me, Mom and Dad would foot the bill."

"He always said it was for you." I smiled and patted his hand, and he grinned.

"Well, my charm is definitely a big factor, no doubt. But if you think about it, our boy doesn't have friends, outside me. He didn't want to room with anyone else, didn't want the competition, maybe? You, Jules, were the most real connection I've seen him make. That's why I was so pissed when he screwed it up. On purpose."

"And it's why he's going to help get you two wacky kids back together again." Ava's eyes flashed bright over Giff's head.

"You know it." He chucked me under the chin, and his cheeks dimpled. "Trust me, kid. We're gonna work it all out."

Chapter Four

I didn't sleep well that night. I was uneasy about Giff's determination to get Liam and me back together, and more than a little guilty about my own plans to throw all that work away in the name of revenge. Liam's feelings didn't worry me; the sting of his very public rejection was still fresh enough that I wouldn't mind tossing some hurt his way. But the idea of deceiving Giff made my stomach turn just a little.

I'd met Giff as soon as I started dating Liam. And looking back, I realized how often he had smoothed things over between us, or taken heat for Liam, deflected blame so that I couldn't be mad. If not for Gifford, Liam and I might not have dated as long as we did. Was that good or bad? I wasn't certain.

"Guess what?" I couldn't contain my excitement, even over the phone, as I dodged other students on the sidewalk.

"Julia, I'm really busy. This project is due tomorrow, and the whole group is dumping the work on me, as usual. Can this wait?"

"No, it can't." I switched ears. *"Remember that article I wrote on how the Civil Rights movement affected Birch? The Inquirer just called Dr. Rawlings. They're picking it up, they're going to publish it next week."*

"Okay."

"Okay? Liam, are you kidding me? This is huge. We're all going out to Roddy's in town to celebrate, the staff and Ava, too. Bring Giff. We'll meet you there."

"Julia, are you listening to me? I can't. I need to get back to work."

Tears of hurt clustered in the back of my throat, and I couldn't say another word. I clicked off the phone and stuffed it deep into my bag, so that I wouldn't be able to hear it if he called back. I shouldn't have bothered; he didn't.

Late the next afternoon, I answered a knock at my dorm room door. Liam stood there with a huge bouquet of flowers.

"So are you still pissed?"

I didn't answer. I leaned against the door jam and raised one eyebrow.

"I'll take that as a yes. Here." He shoved the flowers toward me, so I had no choice but to take them. *"I'm sorry you're mad, Julia. I really didn't have a choice."*

"That's bullshit, Liam. Everyone has a choice. I get you were swamped, and I would have understood that you couldn't come out. But you couldn't be the least little bit supportive? Just a little excited for me?"

He rolled his eyes, and I wanted to hit him. Hard.

"Okay, I get it. I'm a lousy boyfriend. A terrible person.

What else do you want me to say?"

I shook my head. If he didn't understand, there wasn't any way for me to explain.

"Come on." He put one hand on my shoulder. "I made reservations for us at Suzanne's. Get changed, and we'll go celebrate."

I turned and let him follow me into the room, and we went to dinner. And that night I let him make it up to me, as he put it, in bed.

The next day, I ran into Giff coming out of the library as I was going in.

"So did you like the flowers?" He grinned at me. "I know you love orchids. I thought they were perfect."

I closed my eyes. "Did you get the flowers, Giff?"

His mouth drew down, and he blinked. "I—Liam asked me to pick them up, I was going out anyway—it was totally his idea."

"Giff." I patted his arm. "You don't have to cover for him. Liam is..." I looked away, over his shoulder. "Liam is who he is."

I sleep-walked through the first day of classes Monday morning as the professors droned on about syllabi and expectations and class schedules. I liked all of my teachers now; as a junior journalism student, I'd finished all the core requirements and could focus on my major. No more science for liberal arts (which translated to 'science-we're-making-you-take-so-we-look-good-but-you-will-never-use-it')   or math classes, and I wasn't going to miss them.

I trudged through the snow to the car Ava and I shared. Thanks to her shopping trip on Saturday, our trusty Corolla was cleared off and ready to go. I shivered until the heat kicked in and made my way off campus, careful to stick to the slower-than-snail speed limit.

The off-campus roads were snow-free and moving fast. Old Camptown Pike curved over gentle hills and through vast farmland, now showing brown patches where the snow had blown away. The trees were bare skeletons against the bright blue sky.

It was a beautiful day, in spite of the cold, and just being out, driving on country roads with the music blaring, made me feel a little better. I turned off the Pike onto a long driveway that led to a gray stone farmhouse.

I parked the car a little to the side of the garage and made my way across the snow to the side door. I heard voices within as I knocked on the glass.

"Doolia!" A small body slammed into me when the door flew open. "You're back!"

I dropped to my knees, grinning. "Desmond, my favorite boyfriend! I think you grew over Christmas!" His little arms clung tight to my neck, and I buried my nose in his brown curls.

"Des, let Julia come in out of the cold." Sarah's heels clicked into the room. She smiled down at me. "I think he missed you."

"I sure missed him." I rose, still holding his warm three-year old body. "Is it just me, or did he shoot up again?"

She nodded. "I think so. All his pants are short again."

I nuzzled his neck. "You're getting way too big!"

Sarah patted his back. "Which reminds me. Would you be up for a little mall trip?" She dug into the huge red leather purse on the table and pulled out an envelope. "Here's some cash. See if you can find him some jeans, maybe some khakis, if you don't mind."

"Sure, no problem." I hitched Des around to my hip and ruffled his hair. "What else can we do if we go to the mall? Hmm, let me think." I tapped my lip, pretending to be deep in thought.

"Train!" Des wriggled down and ran to his mother. "Mama, Doolia and me gonna go on the train!"

Three-year old boys were so simple and easy. Desmond had two great loves: trains and kittens. The mall gave us a chance to indulge both of those, since we could stop in at the pet store and ride the tot-sized locomotive that snaked around the stores.

Sarah leaned down to kiss his cheek. "Have fun, you two. I'm off. Julia, I'll be home about five or so. Not sure if Danny will make it before me or after, but there's a lasagna in the freezer-if you could stick that in the oven at three seventy-five, I'd appreciate it."

I pulled out a kitchen chair and sat down, pulling Des onto my lap. "Got it. We'll get the shopping out of the way first, yes?" I winked at Sarah over her son's head. "Not that anyone we know would need one, but maybe someone might nap on the way home."

"Not me!" Desmond declared.

"Of course not." Sarah buttoned up her coat. "But Julia looks a little tired, don't you think? Maybe you could tuck her in for a little rest after the mall."

Des looked at me skeptically, and Sarah and I both laughed as she closed the door behind her.

A post-snow, winter Monday spelled a dead mall. Des and I hit the sales racks, and I snagged some good deals on his cute little jeans. We cruised the pet store and shared an ice cream cone before I finally gave into his persistent pleas for a train ride.

After months of weekly train rides, I was intimately acquainted with the elderly man who served as conductor, and he brightened when he saw us approach. I paid for our tickets and helped Des into his favorite caboose seat before folding myself into the tiny space next to him for the thrill-a-minute ride around the wide corridors.

As I had hoped, he conked out on the ride home. I managed to keep him asleep once we got there, and when I was sure he was settled into his toddler bed, I snuggled on the sofa with a reading assignment.

The Flemings home was cozy and comfortable. Dr. Fleming had joined the biology department at Birch last year, and Ava had been in his class when he announced that he and his wife were looking for a part-time nanny. The only caveat was that he couldn't hire anyone whose major was in the sciences, so that he couldn't be accused of favoritism.

Ava, knowing I was looking for a part-time job, passed the info along to me. Sarah and I clicked from our first meeting, and I'd fallen in love with Desmond. And as much as I loved living in the dorm, being in a real home three times a week was definitely a perk of the job.

My night of rotten sleep was catching up with me, and the less-than-scintillating reading for History of Journalism didn't help. I pulled up a wooly red blanket and lay my head back on the pillowed sofa. My eyes drifted close.

I don't know how long I dozed before a slamming door jolted me awake. Disoriented, I bolted upright and grabbed for the baby monitor on the table in front of me. I could hear the steady in-and-out of Desmond's sleeping breath.

Before I had time to look out the window, loud footsteps came from the front of the house. My heart thumped: Danny and Sarah always came in through the kitchen, and I was sure I'd checked all the locks before Des and I left for the mall.

Someone was in the house with me.

I looked around for some kind of weapon, but the Flemings' house was so completely baby-proofed that there wasn't even a heavy knick-knack in reach.

"Hey."

I wasn't sure exactly what I expected an intruder to look like, but it wasn't this. He was tall—or maybe it just seemed that way from my vantage point of cowering on the couch. His light brown hair was wavy, curled at his neck, and his blue eyes were wide with surprise. His worn and faded jeans, along with the flannel shirt just visible under a bulky jacket, didn't quite match the bright red socks on his shoeless feet.

If he hadn't looked so perfectly comfortable standing there, I probably would have thought a homeless man had wandered into the Flemings' family room. He dropped a fat green duffle bag onto the floor and stared at me a moment more.

Instinct kicked in, and I scrambled to the far corner of the sofa, mentally mapping out a path to Desmond's room and praying I could protect the baby.

"Oh, God, I'm sorry." The stranger took one step further into the room and lifted both hands. "I didn't mean to scare you. I mean, I don't know who you are. But obviously no one told you I was coming."

I shook my head, adrenaline still pulsing in my veins.

He came a little closer and stuck out a hand. "I'm Jesse. I'm—Dr. Fleming is my dad."

I opened my mouth to answer when more pounding feet sounded above. Des burst into the room from the other direction, his face still flushed with sleep and his favorite light blue blanket clutched in one arm.

"Doolia, I wake up--" He blinked in my direction and then caught sight of our visitor.

"Big bro!" Desmond launched himself across the room. Jesse scooped him up.

"Little bro!" He hugged the toddler, and all at once I could see the resemblance. Desmond's curls were tighter than his brother's waves, but the color was exactly the same, as was the shape of their faces.

I stood, feeling a little like an intruder as I watched their reunion. Desmond chattered about the train and the snow, and Jesse smiled and nodded in response.

"Hey, dude, so who's this? Is this your girlfriend? How come no one told me you're dating now?"

Desmond giggled as he remembered me for the first time. "Not my girlfriend! Doolia! She's my Doolia." He wiggled, and Jesse set him down on the floor.

Des grabbed my hand and dragged me away from the couch. I smiled, although I was sure my hair was sticking up in all directions and my makeup was probably smudged from sleep.

"Hi, I'm Julia." I would have felt funny extending my hand—and Des had a hold of it, anyway—so I hoped the smile would do. "I hang out with Des while his mom's at work."

Jesse nodded. "I'm sorry for scaring you. I told Dad I'd get here some time today, but maybe they figured it would be later. No one told you I was coming?"

I shook my head. "Sarah was kind of rushed getting out the door, and this was my first day back after Christmas break. She probably just forgot to let me know."

"Hmmm." He frowned, and I wondered if he were upset that no one had thought his arrival important enough to mention to the babysitter. Now that the initial element of terror was wearing off, I remembered a few references to Danny's children from his first marriage. I'd seen pictures of them, a boy and a girl, but looking at Jesse, I realized the photos had to have been over five years old.

"Doolia, I'm hungry!" Des tugged at my hand, and I let him lead me to the kitchen. Jesse followed us, silent as I put a few slices of cheese and apple on Desmond's favorite Thomas the Tank Engine plate.

"So are you here visiting?" I screwed the lid onto the matching cup and set it on the high chair tray. Des grabbed it and chugged like a man just in from the desert.

Jesse slid out a chair and sprawled into it. "No, I'm actually moving here. For a little while, at least."

"Oh. That's nice." *Lame*, I thought. *What a brilliant conversationalist I am.*

"I graduated last year from SUNY, but now I want to get my masters. I was looking at a bunch of schools, and then my dad got this job." He shrugged. "Birch has a decent SLP program, I get a huge tuition break since my dad is a professor, and I can live with him and Sarah rent-free. Call me cheap, but it works for me."

"SLP?" I cocked my head, trying to remember what that meant.

"Speech language pathology. That's my undergrad degree. But you need a masters degree to get a real job, like in a school or a hospital or even working with a practice."

"Oh, that's cool." I reached over to put another piece of apple on Desmond's plate.

"Yeah, I like it. Took a while for me to decide what I wanted to major in, so I was excited when I figured it out." He pulled the package of cheese over toward him, peeled off one slice, folded it and took a bite.

"What about you? Do you go to Birch?" He swallowed and looked at me in question.

"Yeah. I'm in the journalism program. I'm a junior." I wasn't sure why I felt compelled to add that.

Jesse nodded. "So do you live here? I mean, are you like a live-in nanny?"

"Oh, no. I live on campus. I work here three days a week since Sarah went back to work."

"I was just wondering. I'm living in the guest house out back, I guess."

"I haven't been inside it." I played with a napkin on the table, folding it into tiny squares. "So, SUNY? Are you from New York?"

"Yeah, about an hour north of the city. A little town on the Hudson. How about you?"

"I'm a Jersey girl. I grew up on the coast, about an hour from here."

"All done." Des leaned his hands on the tray, struggling to get out of the high chair. "I wanna get down."

"Okay, bub. Hold on." I unbuckled him, wiped off his hands and face and set him free. "There you go. Run wild."

Jesse and I both watched him take off for the toy chest in the corner where he dumped out a bag of wooden blocks.

"You're great with him." Jesse smiled at me. "Do you

babysit a lot?"

"I used to, when I was in high school. I love kids. I have two younger sisters, too. They're 13 and 17 now, but I helped out when they were little."

"Are you the oldest?"

"Yeah. The bossy big sister."

"I'm the middle kid. Or I am now, at least. I have an older sister, and then the little dude." He glanced over at where Desmond was absorbed in his toys. I tried to think of something to say to fill the gap.

"If you ever need someone to show you around the campus or whatever, let me know." *Smooth, Jules.*

He grinned. "Thanks. I might take you up on that. At least you could tell me where the best bars and coffee places are, right? I don't trust my dad to know that."

"Sure, I--" The back door opened on a blast of frigid air, and Dr. Fleming stomped in.

"Jess?" He took the room in two strides and grabbed his son. "You're early. Glad you made it down. How was the drive?"

Jesse hugged him back, and I saw genuine love on his face. "Wasn't bad. Yeah, I made better time than I thought. Scared your babysitter half out of her mind, I think." He gestured to me.

Danny grinned at me, and I was again struck by family resemblance. "Sorry about that, Julia. Sarah must've forgotten to tell you Jesse was coming."

"It's not a problem." I stood up and slung my bag over one shoulder. "Sarah asked me to put on the lasagna, and then I'll head out, unless you want me to stay longer?"

"No, that works. Don't worry about the food, the men

will take care of it." Danny clapped Jesse on the back. "Want to be my sous chef, bud?"

"Daddy, *I* help, too!" Desmond abandoned the blocks to clamor up onto a chair. His dad ruffled his hair.

"Sure, sport, you, too." He smiled at me. "Do you I owe you a check, Julia?"

"Nah, Sarah will take care of it on Friday." I shoved my arms into the sleeves of my coat and glanced at Jesse.

"Nice meeting you. I'm sure I'll see you around, either here or on campus."

"Yeah, definitely." His eyes lingered on me just a minute before Des pulled his attention away.

For the first time in many weeks, I didn't think about Liam once on the way home.

Chapter Five

I didn't see Jesse the rest of that week. When I got to work on Wednesday, Sarah apologized profusely for not warning me that her stepson was expected.

"I completely spaced on that. I'm so sorry."

I shrugged. "No big. I was just a little startled, but Des knew him, so I figured he was legit."

"Oh, yes, Desmond loves his big bro." She smiled at her son as he sat at the table, intent on a coloring page. "He's been in seventh heaven since Jesse got here." Sarah worried her bottom lip between her teeth.

"He seems, um, nice." There was that stupid word again. But what else was I going to say? *Your stepson is really hot?*

"Yeah. Jesse's always been a good kid." She lowered her voice. "You know, it was hard on Danny's older kids when we got married. I mean, Danny and their mom had been divorced for quite a few years before I even met him, but they were used to having him all to themselves. Jesse came around fast, but Alison..." She shook her head. "She's not quite there yet."

"It's really great that you and Dr. Fleming are letting him live here and go to school."

Sarah shook her head. "That didn't take any thought. I love having him around, and of course Danny and Des do, too. And Jesse is awesome with the baby. I wish Alison would come visit more, get to know him better." She sighed and rolled her eyes. "Danny keeps telling me these things take time, and I guess I trust him."

I thought about the Flemings as I hurried through the bitter wind on Thursday afternoon, heading for class. My parents were happily married and still so gooey in love that my sisters and I pretended to be disgusted. But deep down, I knew I was grateful that I didn't have to deal with all the crap I'd seen some of my friends go through. And as much as I liked Sarah, Danny and Desmond, I could see the strain that divorce and remarriage had on the whole family.

Thursdays were my favorite class days, since I only had one two-hour seminar, and it was in the early afternoon. It was my one day to sleep in a little. Plus I was excited about the seminar topic: Modern Journalism and Social Media.

I took a seat in the middle of the large classroom, smiling at a few people I recognized from other classes. By the time we hit junior year, most of us who had been in the same major for two to three years had survived more than a few classes together.

"Hey, you're Julia Cole, aren't you?" The girl sitting behind me leaned forward.

She looked vaguely familiar.

"Yep." I searched my memory for her name but drew a blank. I couldn't even remember what class we might have had together.

"So you dated Liam Bailey. Right? I was at that party last month. You know, his surprise party? My roommate dates a guy on the track team, so they took me along with them. God, that was crazy."

My face froze, and I fell into autopilot. The girl was looking at me in expectation, waiting for a response.

"Umm. Yeah, it was crazy."

"So what did you do? After, I mean? Did you, like, want to beat the shit out of him? Any guy who did that to me, I'd want to kill him."

I shook my head. "No. I haven't even seen him since that night. It's just over." She opened her mouth to say something else, and I added, "And I don't want to talk about it. It's no one's business." I fixed Ms. Nosy Body with a steel glare my sisters used to call the Jules Freeze before I turned around again to face the front.

A few people around us had overheard, and I ignored the murmurs as I opened the fresh notebook and fiddled with my pencil. I was relieved when Dr. Turner appeared a few moments later.

She was a tiny woman with jet-black hair and piercing brown eyes that snapped above the cat-eye glasses she always wore. Once upon a time, she had been part of the Washington press corps and had routinely attended briefings at the White House. She was part of the first wave of women in political journalism and one of my favorite professors; I could listen to her stories for hours.

As always, she launched directly into her lecture, peering at us from time to time over her glasses. Dr. Turner eschewed all the more modern technology; she still used an old overhead projector to share her notes. Today was a class overview, a reiteration of her expectations and rules for those who had never before taken a Turner class and an introduction to our seminar project.

"Now those of you who have had me as a teacher before might recall that I am known for my creative class assignments. This is a new topic. Social media as it relates to journalism has never been taught here before now. So I decided we should be daring and adventurous, try something a little new."

She scanned the room, a little smile playing about her mouth. "I know you all are on the internet and performing what I would term social media experimentations every day. Well, now you get to do it for credit. I want you to take something you're passionate about, some topic that inflames you, something with which you have had personal experience, and for four weeks, devote a blog to this subject. You'll be responsible for promoting each post through other elements of social media that we will discuss in the seminar, and you will present a full report of your modes and methods of operation and all details, due at the final meeting of this seminar."

A low buzz filled the room, and Dr. Turner raised her voice. "All details are in the syllabus you received today. If you have any questions, you know my office hours. And may I just suggest, make your topic specific. Don't bore me with any highbrow crap. I don't want you giving me what you think I'll like. Take something personal. If you have a weight problem, tackle that. If you're struggling with a spiritual issue, that's what I want you to explore. Take the lemons in your life and make them into delicious lemonade."

She clicked off the projector, letting us know that class was over. I closed my notebook and shoved it into my bag, thinking of her words. What kind of lemons could I use for lemonade?

"Julia." The girl from behind me touched my shoulder, and I turned.

"I just wanted to say, I'm sorry about before class. I know it sounded like I was being a bitch, or at least really nosy. But what I wanted to tell you is, I've been there. Guys are jerks. And if you ever need someone, you know, like a shoulder, I promise, I don't have a big mouth."

I smiled. "Thanks. That's really sweet. I'm doing okay." I hesitated a moment. "You said you've been there—you mean—you don't mean with *him*, do you?"

She looked lost for a second and then her face cleared. "Oh, no, sorry. No, for me it was another asshole. A senior I dated when I was just a freshman. He really screwed me over."

An idea was taking root. "I'm sorry, I didn't get your name."

She stuck out a hand. "Kristen. Kristen Howard."

"Good to meet you, Kristen. Do you have time to grab coffee?"

"...so we met at a party, of course, and I didn't find out

he was actually dating someone else until we'd been going out for almost a month. And then he told me that he really wanted *me*, but his girlfriend was fragile, she'd had some kind of addiction, and he couldn't break up with her yet. But he would. And yeah, I was dumb enough to believe him."

We sat in my favorite booth at Beans, each nursing a steaming cup of mocha java. Kristen played with the napkin that lay on the table.

"That's not dumb." I shook my head. "You were a freshman. You liked him. My roommate Ava says trust is our natural state, most of us, at least, so it's not unusual for us to get hurt sometimes."

"Well, maybe. I definitely gave him more than he deserved. I hung on for four months. I let him talk me into sleeping with him. And then he dumped me. His fragile girlfriend came to my dorm room and told me I wasn't the first one he'd used. I don't know why she was willing to stay with him, but she was. I heard they got married after graduation."

I snorted. "Talk about dumb. Why would you tie yourself to a guy you know is a cheater?"

Kristen shrugged. "Right? Maybe she really was fragile. Anyway, that's my story. I haven't dated anyone seriously since then. No big deal. But being at the party last month and seeing what that jerk did to you brought it all back."

I took another sip of coffee. "Did you ever want to do anything to him? You know, like, revenge?"

She laughed. "Oh, believe me, I thought about it. A lot. I just didn't know what I could do that wouldn't end up backfiring on me. I mean, he was a senior, on the football team—did I mention that? And I was just a mousy freshman who was stupid enough to fall in love with him."

"Yeah. I get that." I sighed. "I was thinking about Dr. Turner's assignment. She said to make it personal. So...what if this were my lemon? You know, guys like Liam and your ex. There've got to be other girls out there with stories like ours. What if that were my blog?"

Kristen leaned forward. "That is freaking genius. Do you think she'd let us do a joint one? Would you want to?"

I grinned. "I'd love it. Let's talk to her. Do you have time tomorrow morning? I have to work at noon, but Dr. Turner has office hours at eleven."

"I'm in. I'll meet you there." Her eyes sparkled. "Would it be too corny if I said this might be the beginning of a beautiful friendship?"

Chapter Six

Giff was sitting on the floor outside my room when I got there after my coffee date with Kristen. I stopped short, staring at him until he saw me.

"Oh, hey, Jules." He struggled to his feet and, glancing over my shoulder, raised his voice a little. "I was just waiting to talk with Ava about RA business. Mind if I come inside until she gets back?"

"Umm, sure." I unlocked the door, and Giff followed me inside.

"Sorry about that." He sprawled onto Ava's desk chair. "I didn't want anyone to think I was here to see you."

"Well, thanks. Love you, too."

Giff made a face at me. "You know what I mean. We don't want it getting around that I'm hanging out with you. Liam would think it's weird."

"Again with the flattering."

"Don't you want to know why I'm here?" Giff peeled away his coat and draped it over the end of the bed. "Or would you rather play quippy girl?"

"You mean you didn't come to trade snappy comebacks with me? Damn." I kicked off my shoes and curled up on my bed.

"Tomorrow night. Party at Alpha Delt. Be there at nine."

I sat up so fast I got a head rush. "Oh, no, my friend. No frat parties."

"Why not? And please remember who's in charge here."

"Why not is because I don't do frat parties. I went to one my first week in college, and I sat in a corner while all the other girls got drunk and did things with boys they didn't know. Things I wouldn't do with my boyfriend, if I had one, in the privacy of a very dark room." I shuddered. "Not gonna happen."

Giff sighed, and for a moment he reminded me eerily of Ava. "Jules, you were a freshman, and that was the first week of school. Everyone's a little crazy when they first get here. And Alpha Delt is one of the calmer fraternities."

I flopped back onto my pillow. "Is Liam going to be there?"

"He is."

"Then I really shouldn't go. The idea is for me stay away from him, remember? I distinctly recall you saying that."

"You're not going to see him. Don't worry."

"Then why am I going? Theoretically, I mean."

He grinned at me, those blue eyes sparkling. "He's going to see you. Specifically, he's going to see you leaving the party about the same time he gets there. And you will be leaving with Jack Duncan."

I shook my head. "Again I say to you—I don't think so. Au contraire, mon frere. I know Jack Duncan. I mean, I've heard of him. Do you know what his nickname is? I do. It begins with an 'f' and kinda-sorta rhymes with Duncan."

Giff's lips twitched, but he managed to keep a straight face. "I have heard something about that. But Jack's a good guy. He owes me a favor, and this is it."

The door opened, and Ava came in, shaking water from her head. "It's raining. Last of the snow should be on the way out."

She caught sight of Giff. "Hey, it's the puppet master. What's up?"

"Trying to convince our girl here to go to an Alpha Delt party tomorrow so Liam can see her leave with Jack Duncan."

Ava's brows shot up. "Fuckin' Duncan? No way. Wow."

"Yeah, but Jules isn't impressed."

She swung on me. "Julia, this is perfect. Liam is going to die when he sees you with Jack. Trust us."

I glanced from one face to the next and threw up my hands. "Fine. Whatever. What time should I be there?"

Giff jumped up and hugged me. "Perfect. You won't be sorry. Ava will get you there by eight. You need to be walking out the door with Jack by ten. He knows the drill. Oh, and wear what Ava tells you to put on. She knows the game plan."

He dropped a kiss onto my cheek and put on his coat as he opened the door. "See you later, ladies."

I turned to look at my roommate. "I hope you know what

you're doing."

Ava raised her hands, palms up. "Me? This was your idea. I'm just helping you run with it."

"Well, I think I'm running with it a little more than I'd planned. What do you know about blogs?"

She tilted her head. "Fashion, make-up, book blogs...I follow a few. Why?"

"I'm starting a blog for my social media class."

"Cool." Ava stepped out of her shoes and began to change into sweats. "About what?"

"Guys behaving badly. Girls telling their stories."

"Seriously?" She pulled a green Birch hoodie over her head and shook dark hair out of her eyes.

"Yep. I'm calling it 'Best Served Cold', like the Chinese proverb, you know? Because the girls telling their stories is like getting their revenge."

"Yeah, I got that." Ava considered for a moment and then nodded. "I like it. But how are you going to do it, exactly?"

"We're going to use social media to ask people to share their stories. Anonymously, of course. Then I'm hoping word of mouth will get around."

"What made you decide to start a blog?" She unrolled socks and pulled them on.

I told her about my assignment and meeting Kristen, hearing about her freshman year angst.

"What a jerk." Ava shook her head. "I hear something like that, and I realize why I don't date."

"I thought it was because you had to be single-mindedly focused on academics and then your career until you're established and ready to really have a life."

She flipped me a rude gesture. "You have to admit, boy drama takes up a lot of time and energy."

"It does. Speaking of which, do you seriously think a frat party is a good idea?"

"Yes. This is part of Giff's plan. We go with it. But first, it's your turn to make a run to the dining hall tonight." She stuck her feet beneath the blankets on her bed. "Take an umbrella. It's raining."

It was not only raining, it was a cold, biting downpour. I shivered into my coat and tried to tilt the umbrella so that it kept out the worst of the wet.

The weather matched my mood. I knew Giff wanted to help, and that he was going so far out of his way made me love him even more. But I still wasn't sure I could handle the idea of faking a date with someone I'd never even met, even for Giff.

He'd always been in my corner, I remembered. He kept Liam honest most of the time—even when Liam would rather he kept quiet.

We were all three in their suite. Liam sat at his desk, his nose in a thick textbook, and I was curled up in his bed, reading. Giff sprawled across his own bed, his back against the wall, nursing a beer. It wasn't his first of the evening, and I could hear the slur in his voice, although he wasn't saying much.

I turned over and craned my neck to see my boyfriend. He frowned into his work, and I sighed, wondering why I had bothered to come over at all.

The book I was reading was a love story. I traced a finger over the spine, thinking.

"Liam, why did you ask me out?"

He didn't even look up. "What?"

"When we first started dating. Why did you ask me? You didn't know me at all. What made you do it?"

He finally glanced up, just the faintest annoyance in his eyes. "I don't know, I'd seen you around. I thought you were cute. Why?"

"Just wondering."

"Bullshit."

Giff took a long pull of his beer and repeated the word. "Bullshit. Tell her the truth, Liam. You needed someone to take to that fundraiser with your parents. Your date backed out, you needed another girl. That's why you asked Jules."

I shook my head. "No, that's not right, Giff. Liam never asked me to a fundraiser. Well, not then, anyway."

"No, because he wanted to check you out first, make sure you'd work. But when he asked you out, you said no." Giff lifted his bottle in a mock salute to his roommate. "No one turns down Liam Bailey, so that's when he started chasing you."

"Shut up, Giff." Liam's voice was tight. "You're drunk. You don't know what you're saying."

"Sure I do. You just like to re-write history. Make it how you want. But Jules wants the truth, don't you?" He swiveled his eyes in my direction.

"I just..." I trailed off, uncertain. What had I wanted? Did I really expect Liam to tell me he had been secretly in love with me from afar and finally got up the nerve to ask me

out? I wouldn't believe him, even if he had.

"Julia." Liam's face was tight. "Okay, yes, I needed a date for the fundraiser. But I didn't just pick you because you were convenient. I stood behind you and Ava one day at Beans, and I listened to the two of you. And then I started seeing you around campus. Maybe it was the fundraiser that made me talk to you, but I would have asked you out sooner or later, even if my date hadn't fallen through. All right? We cool? Can I get back to work here?"

I nodded. "Sure."

Across the room, Giff studied me, compassion on his face. Abruptly, he leaned forward, sliding off the bed.

"I need a candy run," he announced. "And I can't go by myself like this. Jules, walk over with to the SU with me?"

I hesitated. It was a week night, but I'd still hoped for some one-on-one time with Liam.

But he waved at me. "Go ahead. I need to finish this chapter, and it'll be easier if I'm alone."

I don't remember what Gifford and I talked about that night as we walked, but I know Giff didn't mention Liam at all. And neither did I.

"*This* is what you want me to wear to a party at Alpha Delt?"

Ava met my eyes in the mirror and grinned.

"Absolutely."

"I don't know, Ave. Are you sure you know what you're doing? You and Giff?" I turned around to face her. "I don't want to look ridiculous. Hell, the last thing I need is more people making fun of me."

"No one's going to make fun of you. Look at the hotness of you."

I rolled my eyes and pivoted to check out the mirror again. My jeans were just faded enough not to look brand new, and the scoop neck black shirt clung in the right places. Still, it was subtle. There wasn't a hint of cleavage, and the jeans weren't even tight. My black boots were flat and cuffed, hardly hot-mama material. I looked more Victorian than vampish.

"Why do you get to wear the cute outfit?" Ava's black skirt was short and flirty. She'd paired it with a slouchy gray sweater that we'd found at a thrift shop before Christmas. The thin knit accentuated her curves and showed more skin than my roommate usually displayed.

"Because I'm not there on a mission. And besides, your outfit is cute, too. But if you dress up all out of character, it's going to look suspicious. Like you're trying to get Liam's attention, not like you just happened to be at a party where he is, too."

"Right. I know." I drew in a deep breath. "Okay, let's go."

It was a still winter night, so cold and clear that the stars seemed very close. I could see our breath as we shivered along the path to fraternity row. Most everyone who lived on campus walked to frat parties since parking was limited in that area, and the campus police tended to patrol more often for DWI on weekends.

I heard music coming from Alpha Delt as we approached, and my stomach turned over. Ava must have sensed it—or heard it—because she grabbed my arm.

"No turning back now," she said, her voice muffled by the scarf wound around her face.

"That sounds incredibly ominous. Like something I'd hear in a horror movie right before zombies pour out of the frat house. Are you sure we shouldn't just go back home, put on our jammies and watch the second season of *Buffy*?"

"Pretty sure. Come on. Man up. Or rather, woman up. Look at it this way. You're getting material for your blog, right?"

"I guess."

Kristen and I had been waiting for Dr. Turner when she arrived at her office that morning. She greeted us with one arched brow as she unlocked the door.

"I assume you ladies have a question about the assignment and that you haven't come to sit at my feet and listen to tales from the stone age of journalism."

I pushed off the wall I'd been leaning against. "I always love to hear your stories, Dr. Turner."

She laughed once, a dry and skeptical sound. "Come in and sit down. Ask your questions."

Dr. Turner was silent as Kristen and I explained what we wanted to do. She was past master at keeping a poker face, and I couldn't read what she was thinking.

When I stopped talking, she drew in a breath and made a steeple of her fingers beneath her chin.

"This is a very interesting topic, ladies. It's the first year we've done the seminar, so I wasn't sure what to expect from my students—maybe a lot of noble causes, possibly some nonsense from the boys...yes, I know, but even in college, boys are less mature, by and large."

I nodded, and Kristen shifted in her chair.

"And I'm not insensitive to the fact that this is a potentially slippery slope you girls propose to tackle. It could easily fall into juvenile male-bashing." She sighed deeply. "But on the other hand, you've both been my students for several semesters, and I flatter myself that I've gotten to know you a bit. I'm going to approve this project. But I want you to be very careful, thoughtful about what you write and conscious of the responsibility you'll bear."

"Thanks, Dr. Turner."

She pursed her lips and leaned back in her chair. "I know I seem like a dinosaur to you girls. But I still remember what it was like. My worst experience in that regard was well after college, but nonetheless..." She shook her head. "Another time."

I thought about her last statement as Ava and I climbed the porch of the Alpha Delt house. There was something comforting about knowing my particular misery wasn't so lonely.

The music pounded around us now, and I winced. Ava shot me an encouraging smile and opened the door.

I had expected the same scene from freshman year, but Giff was right; it wasn't quite as frenetic. People stood in clumps and clusters, sat on the sofas and chairs. It was loud, but not out of control. I recognized a couple of faces, and I was relieved to see that more than one girl wore jeans and sweatshirts. I wasn't going to stick out as much as I'd feared.

We wove our way into the room. A few people greeted us, and I kept out a wary eye for Jack Duncan. I wasn't sure if I was more nervous about the possibility of seeing Liam or the idea that I had to leave the party with Jack.

Ava squeezed my arm and steered me toward the light of the kitchen. A cooler was set up in one corner, next to a table covered with various bottles and plastic cups. A guy stood with his back to us, leaning over a short dark-haired girl. When they heard us come in, he steered the girl around the corner into a darker hallway.

"Not so bad, right?" Ava had to almost yell the words into my ear.

I raised my eyebrows at her and shook my head. "It's loud! And there's people making out or worse on almost every flat surface."

She rolled her eyes at me. "Stop it. Grab a drink and go mingle." Pulling out her phone, she checked the time. "You've got a little more than an hour before we need to be walking out the door with—you know. Try to have a good time, okay?"

I heaved a sigh. "I can't hear myself, let alone you or anyone else. I'm taking my drink outside. Just for a minute."

"All right. Go in the back, looks like they have a deck with space heaters." Ava pointed to a windowed door. "I see someone from my psychology of Shakespeare class. I'm going over to say hello." She picked up a bottle of beer and disappeared into the adjacent dining room.

I found some soda and filled a plastic cup about half way up, leaving out the ice. The amber liquor in a bottle with a pirate picture on the front looked promising, so I added a healthy splash and swished it around. A cautious sip sent delicious warmth down my center, and I smiled. That would do the trick.

I wasn't the only one with the idea to duck outside. Five tall heaters were scattered around the wide wooden deck, and people huddled near them, holding drinks. A few were smoking, but they stood closer to the porch railings.

I made my way to the only unoccupied heater space and concentrated on enjoying the relative silence.

"Julia?"

I turned, startled, as a guy standing at a neighboring heater stepped closer to me. He wore a brown canvas jacket over a green hoodie and carried a cup that matched mine.

"Hey, Jesse." I managed a smile, even though my heart was pounding. *What was he doing here?*

"I was wondering if I might see you tonight." He slugged back his drink and set the empty cup on a nearby chair.

"Yeah, well..." I glanced around. "I don't do fraternity parties, but my roommate dragged me out to this one." I pointed at the door. "She's inside, but it was too loud for me."

Jesse nodded, holding his hands up to the heat. I closed my eyes, cursing inside. *Could I sound any more anti-social?*

"I was an Alpha Delt at SUNY, and my roommate's brother is the fraternity president here at Birch. He asked me to come over tonight. I figured why not, but then I got here. I'd forgotten how much I hated the parties."

I laughed. "Sorry. Why were you in a fraternity if you hate parties?"

"Hey, there's more about frats than parties. I joined because I thought it would look good on my resume, and I wanted to be part of something..." His voice trailed off, and he shook his head. "Okay. Truth is, I joined to meet girls."

"Aha!" I sipped my rum and cola. "And how did that work out for you?"

He shrugged. "I met my share, I guess. I had some fun. But then after a while parties weren't really my thing. I'm more of a talking-and-getting-to-know-you guy than a getting-drunk-and-hooking-up-with-skanks kind of guy."

"Does that imply that I'm a skank, since here I am at a frat party?"

Jesse's eyes widened a bit, and his mouth dropped open. I burst into laughter.

"Kidding. I'm just kidding. I know what you mean. I'm not a hooking-up-drunk girl. I like to hang out with my friends, but this is a little too much, you know?" I circled my hand to encompass the house.

"So why are you here?" He hooked his thumbs in the front pockets of his jeans.

"I told you. My roommate made me come with her. I'm a good friend."

"Yeah." He made an elaborate show of looking all around us. "But where is this alleged roommate? And why did she drag you along and then ditch you?"

"Inside, like I said. Ava didn't ditch me, she just didn't want to come outside in the cold."

"Hmm." Jesse nodded. "Does she date an Alpha Delt? Or does she want to?"

I shook my head. "No. She doesn't date. She's very focused on academics."

He frowned. "So she decided to make you come with her to a fraternity party? Sorry, I don't mean to sound stupid, but I'm confused."

I shifted my weight. I didn't do deception well, and trying to come up with a cover story made me uncomfortable. Jesse was a virtual stranger, but still.

"I don't know. I guess...a friend of ours, well, someone we both know—he invited us. Ava's an RA, and so is he. Anyway, here we are. It's just good to get out sometimes."

"That I get." He grinned, and dimples popped out on both sides of his mouth. My lips may have sagged open. I think I stared. There might even have been drool.

"Hey, Jules?" Ava stood just beyond the door, her arms wrapped around her middle. The guy who stood next to her looked vaguely familiar. He was just a little taller than me, with short hair, muscular arms and wide shoulders.

Yeah, that was Jack Duncan.

Ava looked from Jesse to me, a perplexed frown on her face. And Jack just looked downright confused.

"Ava, this is Jesse. His dad is Dr. Fleming, remember I told you? Jesse, this is Ava, my roommate. And uh, Jack Duncan."

Jesse glanced at me with one eyebrow raised, and I knew he was wondering about Jack. Well, he could keep wondering, because there was no way I was going down that road.

Ava smiled at Jesse and looked back at me, staring hard. "Jack was just looking for you, Jules." She shivered and backed away toward the door. "I'm going back inside...for a little bit. Okay?"

"Sure." I nodded so she'd know I got her meaning. Music spilled out onto the deck as Ava opened the door and disappeared back into the dimness.

And then I was alone with two guys who were both looking at me, wondering what to do or say next.

Jesse moved first. He reached over and offered a hand. "Jesse Fleming. Good to meet you. Are you a Delt?"

Jack's face relaxed. This was familiar territory. "Jack Duncan, yeah. You just visiting or..." He shot me a quick look.

"Grad school. Just started. I was a Delt at SUNY, though. Kyle Martin's brother was my roommate."

"Oh, yeah." Jack nodded. "Kyle's cool."

There wasn't anything else to say, and we all stood there for an awkward moment.

"Jesse's dad is a biology professor, Jack." I had to speak up, finally. "I work for Dr. Fleming and his wife. As a nanny."

"Oh, yeah." Jack pulled out his phone and glanced at the screen. "Sorry, just checking the...a message." He tucked it into his back pocket and turned toward me. "Want to go back inside? I'll get you a drink." His eyes dropped to the cup still in my hand. "A refill?"

I wanted to stand out here and keep talking to Jesse. I wanted to see those dimples again, listen to him talk while his eyes fastened on me. For a split second, I wanted to forget Liam Bailey and the idiotic plan for revenge.

But Jack was staring at me, and I knew he'd agreed to do this as a favor to Giff. Trying to get out of it now wouldn't work. And the truth was, I was chilly, even with the heater.

So I smiled up at Jesse and hoped to hell I'd get another chance with him.

"I guess I'll see you later."

Jack put his hand on my back and steered me inside. I winced at the noise. It must have gone up a few decibels since I'd gone outside earlier.

"What are you drinking?" Jack snagged a beer from the cooler for himself and glanced up at me.

"Um. Rum and cola." I held out my cup. "No ice, please."

The soda was flat, but I didn't say anything. Jack added the rum and passed me the cup. He lifted his beer in a half-hearted sort of toast.

"Here's to...shit, I don't know. New friends?"

I couldn't help smiling. Jack Duncan wasn't my type, not even a little, but so far he seemed to be a pretty good sport.

"Sure. New friends. And favors."

He touched the bottle to my cup and took a long swig. "We've got about twenty minutes." He leaned toward me and kept his voice low, though how anyone could hear us over the thump of the music was beyond me. "I figured we should hang together, look, um, close, in case someone asks questions."

Jack's warm brown eyes were serious, and I bit my lip to keep from laughing. He was taking this whole situation very seriously. I wondered what Giff had told him.

We ended up sitting at the table, sipping our drinks and talking as well as we could over the bass. The few times that people passed through the kitchen or came in to refill their drinks, Jack touched my hand, leaned closer to me or draped one arm behind my chair.

Ava appeared in the doorway just as Jack and I were laughing at a football story he was telling me. She caught my eye and tapped her wrist.

"I think that's our cue." I stood, pushing the chair back. I wasn't sure if the dizziness I felt was the rum or the idea that if all went as planned, Liam would see me in a few moments.

I followed Jack into the living room and dug through a pile of coats until I found mine. He pulled on a worn letterman's jacket. Wrapping one arm around my waist, he moved toward the door.

Jack's eyes scanned the yard as we stepped outside into the still and frigid air. I saw him focus on two figures moving across the grass. He grasped my upper arms and backed me against the wall of the porch.

"This is improv," he whispered into my ear. "Just go with it. Be a vixen."

"A *vixen?* What is--"

Before I could say any more, Jack was kissing my neck, and his hands were under my coat, on my ribs. I heard footfalls on the porch just as Jack spoke again, this time loud enough to be heard.

"Julia, c'mon. Let's go back to my room." He trailed his fingers down my arm and tugged on my hand. I had no choice but to stumble forward into him.

Out of the corner of my eye, I caught sight of Giff's blond head. I knew Liam was standing next to him, but I didn't let myself look. My heart was pounding, and meeting those familiar eyes just might break me.

Jack had his arm twined around me as we moved to the steps. He raised one hand in Giff's direction.

"Hey, dude. Where you been? Missing an awesome party." There was a slur in his voice that I was pretty sure was more acting, since I'd only seen him nurse one beer over the last hour.

"Yeah, looks like it." Giff's voice was arch with meaning. If I hadn't known he was in on this plan, his tone would have hurt.

"You okay to drive, Jack?" My breath caught. That was Liam speaking, the first time I'd heard his voice in nearly two months. He didn't sound jealous or angry, but possibly just a tad...concerned. About me? Maybe.

"Not driving, we'll walk." Jack pulled me down another step. "Later, man."

I didn't want to leave. Liam was on that porch, and even though I knew I didn't love him, even though he'd humiliated me, bruised my heart, I still wanted to be near him. I wanted to slap him, but at the same time, I wanted to wrap my arms around his waist and feel him lay his cheek on the top of my head, as he always did. I craved that feeling of security like a drug, even if the security Liam had offered me had been a total illusion.

But I couldn't go back. Jack was much stronger than me, and he was dragging me along. He didn't stop until we hit the sidewalk.

"You okay?" His voice was gruff, and I sensed I was making him very uncomfortable. I didn't know why. And then I felt the trickle of tears down my cheeks.

"I'm sorry." I tried to say it, but instead, I was sobbing. Jack pulled me to him, and I wept against his solid chest.

"Hey, c'mon. Don't do that. Crying freaks guys out."

I half-laughed through my tears. "I know. I didn't mean to, I'm really sorry. It just—I hadn't seen him since—and I guess it was harder than I thought."

"Yeah, guys are assholes." Jack said it with such cheery assurance that I laughed again, wiping at my face as I pulled away from him.

"Jules, what's wrong?" Ava was at my side.

"Where'd you come from?" I glanced around, but no

one else stood near us.

"I went out the back and circled around after I saw Giff and Liam come in. Did he say something to you?" I heard the anger in her usually calm voice.

"No. No, he didn't say anything." I took a deep breath to stave off another round of tears. "And Jack was freaking amazing."

In the dim light coming from a street lamp, Jack grinned. "I was, wasn't I?" He lowered his voice, though there was no one nearby to hear. "Don't tell anyone, but I take drama classes. In town. I'm part of a club. That's where Giff and I got to be friends."

"Well, color me impressed." I patted his arm. "You rocked that. You sounded like you were drunk, and I'm sure it looked like we were making out on the porch."

"Yeah." He stood back a little and looked me over, up and down. Although I'd felt safe and comfortable with him up to now, I felt a whole different vibe as he checked me out.

"You know, you ever want to get together for real, no audience..." He let his words trail off, but the suggestion was obvious. I moved closer to Ava.

"Thanks, Jack, and I really do appreciate you doing this tonight, but I think we're probably meant to be friends." I ventured close enough to just kiss his cheek. "You just might be too much man for me."

He smirked and nodded. "Yeah, could be. Okay, you girls all right to get back to your room, or you want me to walk you? I'm going to another party in town."

"We're good. Thanks, Jack." Ava answered for us, and Jack sketched a wave as he jogged off in the other direction.

Ava turned to me. "Want to stop at Beans?"

I pulled my coat tighter around me. "Let's go back to the dorm. I don't think I can handle anything else tonight. Being a vixen is exhausting."

Chapter Seven

I spent most of the weekend catching up on homework and setting up our new blog. Kristen came over to help me, and I was grateful for her expertise.

"I had an idea." She was sitting on the floor, shoes off and legs tucked beneath her. "What if we made a Facebook page for our blog, and that's where we put out the word about wanting girls' stories? Between that and word of mouth, it could give us a decent start."

"Sounds good. And I talked to Amy. She'll run an ad for us on-line, saying we're collecting stories for research purposes. No names, of course—ours or theirs." Our school newspaper had gone paperless two years before, and Amy, who was now the editor, had been a driving force in that move. I'd worked with her since my freshman year.

"What is your goal with this blog?" Ava turned around

from her desk, studying us. "What do you hope to accomplish?"

Kristen and I looked at each other. "I guess...just raising awareness. Giving girls an outlet for telling what happened to them."

"It made me feel better to know I wasn't the only one this happened to, when I talked to Kristen. So maybe it can be helpful to others in that way, too."

Ava nodded. "That makes sense. You might want to think about promoting it to the guys, too. Seeing the fallout wouldn't hurt them."

"Good point." I made a note. "We need to keep it all anonymous. I don't want anyone sending us hate mail."

"True." Kristen stood and stretched. "I'll work on the blog set up tonight. You'll write the intro, the first post?"

"Sure." I walked with her to the door and jumped back as Giff stood there, his hand raised to knock.

"Whoa." He looked nearly as startled as me. "Didn't know I was expected."

"You weren't." I pulled him into the room. "Giff, this is my friend Kristen. Kristen, Gifford Mackay."

Ava stood up. "Did you bring those forms back to me, Giff?"

"Um, yeah." Giff glanced at Kristen and then at Ava. "But can I talk to you about them first?"

I gave Kristen a bright, on-your-way smile. "Okay, well, see you in class Thursday! Text me if anything comes up with the project."

She nodded, looking more than a little mystified as she left. I shut the door behind her with a sigh. My life was getting way too complicated. Giff couldn't know about the blog, and Kristen didn't have the full story on Giff's let's-get-these-crazy-kids-back-together scheme. And neither of them knew about my revenge plans. It was exhausting.

"So." Ava pushed Giff into her desk chair and sat down on her own bed. "Tell all. Did Liam say anything about Jules and Jack last night?"

Giff grinned, not a little smugly. "He definitely saw them. He wasn't happy, but he was being cool. He asked me later if I'd heard anything about you and Jack. I played dumb."

"What did he say, exactly?" I knew I was torturing myself, but I had to know.

"He said, 'So, Duncan and Julia? When did that happen?' And when I told him I didn't know, I hadn't heard anything, he said, 'I hope she knows what she's doing. He's out of her league.'"

I frowned. "'Out of my league'? What is that supposed to mean?"

Giff shrugged. "Come on, Jules, you said it yourself the other day. Jack's got a rep. Anyone who hangs with him is going to get one, too." He winked at me. "Sorry, kiddo. If you're going through with this, your halo may take some dings."

I winced. Dating Liam had taken me out of obscurity in the social microcosm that was Birch College. The way he'd dumped me had given me a certain level of notoriety, but still, most people didn't know who I was. I wasn't sure I didn't like that.

"Are you ready for our next adventure? I promise this one is easier."

"I'll be the judge of that. What is it?"

Giff spread out his hands. "Eating dinner in the dining hall. Something you should be doing anyway."

"And...?" I raised an eyebrow.

Giff sighed. "Well, you'll be eating with some company. Three guys from the football team."

I dropped my head into one hand. "Giff, really? And I have a question. How are you getting these guys to help us? I'm starting to worry about you and your favor system. Jack really took his job seriously. What did you promise him? Or threaten him with?"

He shook his head. "That's not for you to worry about. Hey, I'm a nice person, and I'm very popular, you know. I do favors. Help people out. So they're more than happy to do the same for me."

"Hmmm." I remained unconvinced. "But what happens after this? How many times will I have to show up in public with a different guy before Liam cracks? If it even works."

"Jules, did you expect him to fall at your feet and beg for forgiveness the first time he saw you with another guy?" Ava smiled.

"A girl can hope. If he really missed me..." I shook my head. "No. I didn't. But I have to be honest, Giff. I don't think this is going to work. I could parade all over campus for months with every guy you know, and if Liam isn't interested, it won't make a difference. Except at the end, I'll be known as the biggest slut at Birch."

"Hey, hey, I said your halo might take some dings. I'd never let anyone call you a 'ho." Giff looked affronted. "And after this dinner, you won't have to do anything for a while. I have some people who are set up to talk about you." He reached across and patted my knee. "Don't worry, they won't be saying anything bad. Just dropping your name here and there. Along with other names. In a positive way."

"Giff, have you considered going into public relations?" Ava had her scheming eyes on. "You'd be a natural."

"Eh, poli sci, PR, same difference. I'll just be spinning shit on a national level instead of for celebs." He stood and squeezed my shoulder. "And you can say you knew me when. Right?"

"Assuming I live through this, sure."

Giff rolled his eyes. "Oh, the melodrama. Seriously, Jules, leave that to me. I do it so much better." He slung a bright red scarf around his neck. "Now if you lovely ladies will excuse me, I have a date tonight."

"Really? Do we know him?" I smiled in spite of myself. Giff made me uneasy at times, no question, but I still loved him to death.

"Nope, I doubt it. And I don't want to say any more, 'cause I might jinx it."

"Have fun, be safe!" Ava called as he closed the door with a parting wave.

I curled up on my bed, tucking one hand beneath the pillow. Outside it was gray and dreary, matching my mood.

"Shakespeare had it right," I murmured.

"Of course he did, but about what, in particular?" Ava had taken a book into bed with her and mirrored my position, snuggled under the covers.

"Weather reflects the human condition."

"Oh, yup. That's true. So you're feeling gloomy?"

"I guess."

"Hmm." She rolled to her back and propped the textbook on her stomach. I closed my eyes and tried not to think about blogs or ex-boyfriends. Just as I was about to doze off, Ava spoke again.

"That guy you were talking to Friday night. Dr. Fleming's son? He's cute."

I sighed. "He really is. And you didn't even see the dimples."

"There were dimples?"

"There were."

"Oh, man." She shifted, punching her pillow and bunching it under her head. "You seemed like you were getting along when Jack and I interrupted."

I groaned and pulled the covers over my head. "He probably thinks I'm insane. I got all flustered when you guys came out. And then I went off with Jack, without explaining anything. I mean, what could I tell him?" I squeezed my eyes shut. A headache was beginning to form in my temples. "Just one more person thinking I'm nuts."

"Jules, you know, you can call this off any time. Tell Giff to cease and desist."

"I know. But...I'm not ready yet. When I saw Liam Friday night—well, when I didn't see him, when I heard him—that hurt felt all new and shiny again. If he had looked at me, Ave, if he had just said my name, I'm afraid I would have gone right back to him. I want to get over that."

"Okay." Her voice was gentle. "Just know, I'm behind you, whatever you want to do."

"Julia..."

I had dozed off, and Liam's voice in my ear brought me around. I smiled, my eyes still closed.

"Time to wake up."

I snuggled closer to his warmth, breathing in his scent. "Don't want to."

He laughed, and I heard it deep in his chest. Desire surged low within me. I crept my fingers up to trace his pecs, trail down to his stomach.

Liam sucked in his breath as I moved lower. He caught my hand just as it skimmed the waistband of his shorts.

"We're supposed to go to that brunch. You're not helping me want to go."

"Hmm. What time is it? Did the alarm ring?"

"About half an hour ago. You turned it off." He brushed his lips across my ear, and I shivered.

"Why didn't you wake me up before?"

"I was enjoying the view." He moved his mouth to my shoulder, inching the blanket lower, and I remembered I had slept without anything on. Warmth spread from my face even lower.

Ava was away for the weekend, at some sort of conference for psychology students. It had been a huge honor for her to be selected to represent Birch, and I was thrilled for her, but I was even happier that she was in St. Louis for four days, giving Liam and me rare nights alone.

"Remind me why we're getting out of bed to eat some lousy food?" Liam's hands had joined his mouth, and I gasped as he fastened on my breast.

His tongue circled the nipple before he spoke. "Plans made before I knew Ava was going to be gone. God, you're beautiful." He shifted, moving on top of me, and I could feel that we weren't getting out of bed any time soon...

I woke with a gasp, my heart beating in my ears and my body flushed. I hadn't dreamt of Liam often in the past few months, and mostly it was nonsense, crazy stuff without rhyme or reason. But this had been a memory, so real I nearly turned in bed and reached for him.

The dream stayed with me for the rest of the day. I was preoccupied, and every nerve was close to the surface. I nearly rear-ended the car in front of me on the way to work.

"Are you okay?" Sarah peered at me, a frown etched on her face. "You look...not right."

"Ah, just a late night. School work, I mean." The Flemings had met Liam while we were dating and were aware that we had broken up, but I hadn't shared details. Although my social life or lack thereof wasn't a subject we ever discussed, I still didn't want my employers thinking I was out partying all the time.

"You sure you're not coming down with something?" Sarah didn't look convinced.

"No. I mean, yes, I'm sure." I stooped down and picked up Desmond. "Nothing a little Des love won't take care of." I nuzzled his sweet baby neck.

"Okay, then." Sarah put on her coat. "I have a late consult, and then I'm meeting Danny for dinner. So Jesse is going to take over on Des duty at five." She leaned over and gave her son a smacking kiss. "Love you, baby boy. Be good for Julia."

"Wove you, too, Mommy!" He waved as Sarah shut the door behind her.

"Want to build with some blocks, buddy?" I set Desmond on his feet and followed him to the toy corner. He dumped the bin onto the tile floor with a crash, and I sat down cross-legged to help him create.

Knowing I was going to see Jesse later gave me a warm buzz. I crossed paths with him now and then here at his dad's, though I'd yet to see him on campus since our chat at the fraternity. He stopped into the house to see Des or raid the fridge, but he never hung out with us very long. He kept things friendly with me, but just a tad aloof, and I wondered what he might have heard about me at the frat party.

Probably better, I thought with an inward sigh. *Those dimples are deadly.*

When nap time came, it took four books to lull the three-year old to sleep, and I very nearly joined him, snuggled up to his sturdy warmth. My eyes were almost closed when I heard a door close downstairs.

I eased away from Desmond and slipped down the steps. As I turned the corner, I saw Jesse in the kitchen, taking off his coat and hanging it over a chair.

"Hey." I spoke just loud enough for him to hear me, but still, he turned, startled.

"Oh, hi, Julia." He glanced around and then lowered his voice. "Is the munchkin sleeping?"

"Yeah, I just got him down." I shoved my hands into the pockets of my jeans and rocked back on my heels a little.

"Cool. Sarah said you stay until five, right? I know he's sleeping, and if you need to take off, go ahead, but I'd like to get some work done if you don't mind hanging out."

"I planned to be here until then anyway, so that works." I pointed to the pan on the stove. "I made Des mac and cheese for lunch. You want some before I put it away?"

Jesse grinned. "Mac and cheese, my favorite. You going

to have some, too?"

I hadn't been hungry earlier, but scooping the pale yellow noodles onto a plate for Jesse made my stomach rumble. I pulled out another plate and zapped both servings in the microwave before setting them on the table.

We ate in silence for a few minutes. I had expected tension or at least awkwardness, but it was actually quite peaceful and comfortable.

"Did you make this from scratch or from a box?" Jesse swallowed another huge mouthful.

"Please. A box? Don't insult me."

He raised his eyebrows. "I'm impressed. It's delicious." He forked another few noodles. "I don't know many people who cook. My mom, she can't even boil water. And my sister lives on junk food and take-out."

"Sarah cooks," I pointed out. "I mean, I guess she does. She always has, like, casseroles or something in the freezer for me to put in the oven."

"She does okay, but she doesn't like it. When she and my dad first got married, she tried to cook for Ali and me. She did pretty well on the basics, but her cookies and cakes—not so much."

"My mother writes cookbooks." I played with the cheese residue on my plate. "So I've been surrounded by food my whole life. I have two sisters, and we all kick ass in the kitchen."

"And modest, too." Jesse grinned, and there they were. The dimples had come out to play again. I was struck by the sudden and almost irresistible urge to cover them with my mouth and trace them with my tongue...

"Hey, you okay? You checked out there for a minute."

He was looking at me with narrowed eyes. I hoped my mouth was closed.

"Sorry. Yeah, modest. Well, I don't have many obvious talents, so what I know I can do, I like to celebrate."

"I don't know. You're good with kids, clearly, 'cause Des loves you. He talks about you all the time. And you're a journalism major, right? So I bet you're a good writer. Plus, you're really pretty, and if you can cook, too? Those are some fairly major talents."

"Wait, wait, wait." I held up one hand. "Did you just call me pretty?"

Jesse's eyes widened, and he got a deer-in-the-headlights look. "Yeah, I guess that's not really a talent. Wow, my sister would be calling me a sexist pig if she were here. Sorry."

"No, that's not what I meant. You think I'm pretty?"

He smiled again. "Well, yeah. Why are you acting like that's big news?"

I lifted one shoulder. "A girl doesn't hear that often enough. At least I don't. So thanks."

"I find that hard to believe. I saw the way guys were looking at you Friday night. And that Jack you left with, he must tell you. Or if he doesn't, he should."

I'd been waiting for Jack's name to crop up. "Jack's just a friend. I don't even know him that well." Telling the truth about that much was a relief.

"I think he wants to be more. He was kind of intense."

I couldn't help laughing. "Well, umm...it's a secret, but Jack is taking drama classes, and he was practicing Friday night. He doesn't care about me."

"I'd say those classes are paying off. When you left, I

would have sworn you were at least close friends."

So he'd noticed, and enough that he'd thought about me. The idea gave me a warm glow.

"Did you have fun Friday night?" A slight change in subject was in order.

Jesse picked up his plate and carried it to the sink. "I didn't stick around very long after I talked with you. Like I said, parties aren't my thing and it was a long week. I came back here and watched *Firefly*."

"Really?" I followed him to the sink and waited for him to finish with the water. "I wanted to stay home and watch *Buffy* instead of being at the party. So I'm kind of jealous."

"*Buffy*...yeah, now that was television." Jesse slid his plate into the dishwasher rack and held out his hand. "Give me your plate."

"What? Oh, no, that's okay, I'll clean it."

"Nope, you cooked, I clean. Gimme."

I acquiesced and leaned against the counter. "That's a very evolved attitude."

"That's me, evolved. I grew up around a lot of women. I know my place." He ran the water again and scrubbed at the leftover cheese. "So you're a Joss fan?"

"Are you kidding? Joss Whedon is a freaking genius. I'd watch anything he wrote or produced."

"Yeah, me too. I just got *Dollhouse* on DVD."

"Another one of my favorites." I watched Jesse's muscles roll beneath his snug t-shirt as he reached down to the dishwasher again and then turned to dry his hands. He didn't mention playing sports, but he was definitely built.

He caught me staring, and one side of his mouth lifted, followed by one dimple. I swallowed hard.

"So did you see *Much Ado About Nothing*?"

I cocked my head. "The play? Yeah, I've seen it a few times. I'm kind of a Shakespeare nerd."

"No, I meant Joss's film of it. Don't tell me you haven't heard of it."

"Joss did Shakespeare? I'm a loser. I didn't know. Guess I'll have to see it on DVD."

Jesse hooked his thumbs in the belt loops of his jeans. "It came out last summer, but it's still playing at the dollar theater in town. You really should see it on the big screen." His eyes were holding mine, steady but tentative.

I nodded. "I guess I really should."

He licked his lips. "Would you want to go see it? This weekend, Friday, maybe?"

A tingle danced down my spine. "With you?" I knew it sounded dumb, but I wanted to be sure what he was asking.

"Well, yeah, with me. I mean, if you want."

I bit the side of my lip. "I would love to. But I'm not sure it's a good idea."

He frowned. "Why not?"

I ticked off the reasons on my fingers. "First, I work for your dad. I don't want to make anyone uncomfortable. And second..." I looked down at the floor. "My life is kind of complicated right now. I just got out of a relationship. It was messy. And ugly. I don't want to drag you into the drama."

Jesse didn't answer me right away. He seemed to be staring at the same spot on the floor that held my attention.

"But you're not seeing anyone now? The messy relationship is over?"

"Oh, yeah. Way over. But the guy was high-profile on campus, and..." I shrugged. "People talk."

"Okay. But no one here knows me. We'll stay off campus, if you're worried about people seeing you with me."

"It's not you. I don't care about that. But maybe you don't want to be seen with me."

One side of his mouth lifted in a half-smile. "Let me worry about that. And I'm not."

I took a deep breath. "All right. Let me think about it. I'm not saying no."

"But you're not saying yes, either?"

"Not yet. But ..." I smiled. "I really do love Joss, and Shakespeare, too, so chances are pretty good I'll change my mind."

He nodded. "Where's your phone?"

I reached into the back pocket of my jeans. "Right here. Why?"

"Give it to me." He took it from my hand and hit a few buttons. "There. Now my number is programmed in, so when you do change your mind, you can text me." He hit another button, and I heard a buzzing. "And now I just called myself from your phone, so I have your number, too. So I can text you and remind you to change your mind." He handed me back my phone.

"Thanks."

"I better get to work on that paper. Thanks for the mac and cheese." He put his hand on the door knob but hesitated before turning it. "I hope I'll see you Friday night.. And for the record..." He turned and flashed the duet of dimples.

"You really are very pretty."

Chapter Eight

I think I floated home from work that night. I grinned stupidly every time I thought of Jesse, especially when I remembered that he told me I was pretty.

I didn't have an inferiority complex. I knew I wasn't a complete troll, but I also was well aware that I didn't measure up to what guys considered hot. Dating Liam had been a big ego boost, sure, but he hadn't been the most reassuring boyfriend ever, either. The only time he really gave me compliments or praise was when we were in bed, and in my mind, that didn't count.

But Jesse was different. The conversation we'd had that afternoon was more in-depth and real than any talk I'd ever had with Liam. I liked the way his mind worked, and he seemed to be interested in many of the same things I was. While I wasn't ready to jump into anything again—I was still wary of all things guy—Jesse intrigued me.

"Well, you look more alive than you did this morning. You must have gotten a good nap at Dr. Fleming's house." Ava smiled at me as I danced into our room.

"Nope, no nap. But I did hang out with Jesse Fleming, and guess what I just might have?"

Ava's brows drew together. "I'm thinking something in the pharmaceuticals area, the way you're grinning."

"Not even close. I might have a date. For Friday night. With Jesse Fleming."

"A *date*?" Ava left the desk and sat down on her bed. "How did that happen?"

"I'm not really sure. He came home while Des was sleeping, and we ate mac and cheese and talked, and then he asked me to the movies with him on Friday."

"Jules, that's awesome." She jumped up and gave me a brief, tight hug. "I know you need this. And like I said, he's cute."

"He is. But he's, like, a decent person, too. He's someone I could be friends with even if he wasn't sexy and didn't have those adorable dimples." I paused. "He's the kind of guy I kept wishing Liam was the whole time we were dating."

"Oh, sweetie." Ava patted my arm. "I know. But why do you keep saying you *might* have a date? He asked, you said yes, so...?"

"I didn't say yes yet. I'm not sure if I should. Between Giff's plans and mine, maybe bringing someone else into the mix is a bad idea."

"Jules, this whole idea was about you moving on. This could be a sign that you can. That you should."

"I know. But I'm not ready to let this go. Maybe I should be, but it still comes down to the same thing in my mind. I want Liam to understand what he did to me. Dating someone else doesn't negate that."

Ava nodded. "I understand. Well, if you do go out with Jess and Giff finds out, you can always just say you found someone else to help make Liam jealous."

"True." I sat down at the desk and opened my laptop. "Wow. Look at this. Since Anne posted that ad for us about the blog, we've gotten a ton of submissions. And comments."

"And I saw the Facebook page that you and Kristen put up is getting some interest. A few people posted on there, too."

"I see that. So far, all we're getting is the classic boy-done-girl wrong tales."

"What were you expecting? Isn't that what you wanted?" Ava rolled her shoulders, stretching.

"Yeah, I guess so. Maybe I wanted to hear a little more. I want to know why the guys do this. What makes a boy think it's okay to treat a girl so badly?"

Ava laughed. "That's a question women have been trying to answer for centuries. Good luck, sister."

I sighed, getting down to work on the blog. "Thanks."

Over the rest of the week, in between putting together the stories for the project and keeping up with the rest of my schoolwork, I fielded texts from Jesse. He started fairly low-key with a simple 'hello' here and there, checking in, asking what I was doing. But he usually worked in a reminder about the movies on Friday night.

Are you still thinking?

I do it all the time.

Smartass. About the movie. Friday. Me.

I smiled. I hadn't been able to stop thinking about it—about him.

Oh, that?

Yeah, that. Are we on?

Hmmm

That's not a no.

It's a hmmm.

C'mon. It's just a movie.

I was ready to give in, ready to type those three letters he wanted to see—YES. My fingers were poised over the keys.

"Jules."

Ava stood in our open door, just back from class. It was a rare mild day, and she was carrying her coat instead of wearing it.

"Sorry, didn't want to startle you. Looked like you were preoccupied there." She pointed to my phone. "God, it was nice out today. Spring is in the air." She dumped her backpack on the desk. "And you have dinner plans."

"I do? No, I don't." I glanced up from my phone again. I still hadn't answered Jesse's last text.

"I ran into Giff on the way over here and agreed to deliver a message. Be at the dining hall at six. I'll go with you. He told me which table we need to sit at, and then your dates will arrive. He said to tell you to be flirty and friendly, but not over the top."

"Oh, God." I rolled my eyes and groaned. "Seriously?"

"Yeah. Liam is supposed to be there around the same time. I'm allowed to sit with you, but I can't appear to be with any of the guys."

"Of course not. Did he tell you how I'm supposed to dress? What is it this time, sweats?"

"No, he said just wear whatever you want, but nothing special. Don't look like you're trying to catch Liam's attention."

"Because Liam always paid so much attention to how I dressed," I muttered.

"Jules, either commit to this, or don't. The whole plan was your idea. Like I told you before, if you're uncomfortable, shut it down. But don't act like Giff is forcing you into anything. He isn't. He's trying to be helpful."

"I know. I'm being a bitch. He's a good friend, and you're wonderful, and I'm a pain in the ass. I'm sorry. I think...I'm scared. I'm afraid you and Giff are going to all this trouble, and Liam isn't going to care. What if he doesn't, Ave? What if he's just glad that he doesn't have to deal with me anymore? And what's wrong with me, that *I* care?"

Ava, being Ava, didn't rush to tell me I was wrong. She frowned, started to say something, and then stopped.

"You think that's true, don't you?" I closed my eyes. "I'm doing all of this crazy shit to get him back just to dump him, and it won't mean anything to Liam. I'm an idiot."

"No, that's not exactly what I was going to say." Ava looked over my shoulder, as though trying to focus on something just beyond my face. "I think...I think maybe it will work out. At least, it will work as far as Liam might think he wants you again, and you'll get the chance to toss it back in his face."

"And...?" I knew there was more by her expression.

"And maybe he'll learn something about how to treat girls. Or maybe...he'll find out that he's relieved that you don't really want him, either."

I sucked in a breath and leaned back against the wall. "Okay. Ouch, I think."

"I knew that was going to come across wrong. No, listen to me. What have you been saying all along, since Liam broke up with you? That you didn't really want to date him in the first place, right? Sweetie, we know you were never really in love with him. You liked dating him. Being Liam Bailey's girlfriend, when no one else had been able to hold him for more than a few weeks. And whether you want to admit it or not, you liked the sex."

My face burned, but I didn't deny it, the memory of my dream earlier in the week still fresh in my head.

"So maybe...it could have been the same with him. He liked you, definitely loved the sex--what guy wouldn't— liked that his parents approved of you. But you know, the whole time you two were together, I got the sense that he wasn't quite...committed. He was always holding back. Remember the other day, when you were talking about Jesse, you said he was the guy you wished Liam had been?" She bit her thumb, still not meeting my eyes. "To be honest, I wasn't surprised that he broke up with you. I hated how he did it, yes, and I think he's a jerk, but I also think he did the right thing. He just did it in a dick way."

I closed my eyes, thinking about Ava's words. She wasn't wrong, and if I were being straight with myself, I'd admit I had thought the same thing. Or at least along the same lines.

"So why are you going along with me, helping me do

this?"

Ava smiled. "Because I do love you, and I believe you need this on some level. And maybe because I think in the long run, it'll be good for Liam, too, though he might not agree right away."

I bit the side of my lip. "All right, then. To the dining hall?"

"Absolutely. Just let me pull my hair back." She vanished into the bathroom.

Jesse probably thought I was blowing him off. I opened his last message again.

Sorry about that. My roommate just came in. Have to go now, promise I will answer you tonight.

I opened my closet and found my favorite hoodie, a pale green fleece with the name of my high school embroidered on the front. The color set off my skin tone and hair and brought out my eyes. Or at least that was what my mother told me. I just loved it because it was warm and unbelievably comfortable.

Ava and I didn't often eat at the dining hall. Our eating plan was part of Ava's RA deal, but we could use our meal credits at the student union food court as well as the main hall. And since the food court allowed us to get take out, we usually opted for that choice.

The sun set as we made our way across campus to the brick building. The relative warmth of the day was giving way to the evening chill, and I hugged my arms tighter around my middle, glad I had put on gloves.

We went through the check-in line and picked up trays. Ava sighed in defeat. "What makes them think that someone is going to want tacos every night of the week? The smell makes me want to puke."

"I don't think they expect the same person to eat a taco every night. More like, someone on campus is going to crave Mexican. But I agree. Salad bar?"

"Definitely."

We loaded our plates with vegetables and cheese, dug bottles of water from the cooler, and then I followed Ava to a round table in the middle of the room, right along the main walkway.

"Are you sure this is the one Giff meant?" I glanced around. My choice would have been tucked back in one of the dark corners.

"Positive. Sit down." Ava dropped her tray onto the table and pulled out a chair. I followed suit.

"How long do you think we'll have to..." My voice trailed off as three men in sweats and t-shirts approached the table, identical expressions of determination on their faces.

"Hey." Their trays clanked on the table, nearly in unison. I was surrounded by almost-overwhelming testosterone.

They were all big guys with the thick necks I'd come to associate with football players. Their hair was buzzed short, and their t-shirts revealed muscle-knotted arms. I swallowed hard, my throat suddenly very dry.

"You're Julia, right?" The one sitting closest to me leaned over and spoke low. "Giff said long brown hair, sitting with a short Italian girl with black hair." He looked at Ava.

"Nice to know how my friends describe me." She rolled her eyes.

"Yes, I'm Julia." I smiled, conscious that Liam could be

in the dining hall watching us even now. "But Giff didn't tell me your names."

"I'm Phil, that's Kent and this is Marcus." Phil's eyes ran up and down me, taking in the hoodie and jeans. "You're pretty cute."

"Oh, thanks. That's nice of you." I lay my hand on his arm and fluttered my eyes. "How do you all know Giff?"

They exchanged looks around the table. "Uh, just around. Kent went to high school with him and—you know, Bailey."

"Yeah, Giff was on the football team back then." Marcus spoke around the huge stuffed taco he was cramming into his mouth.

"You're kidding." Ava had been quiet until now. "I didn't know that."

"Yeah, he'd played since he was a kid. He can move, you know. He got hurt when we were sophomores, and then after that he went into being the kicker. Got a decent leg."

"So why doesn't he play now?" I turned to Kent, trying to keep it all even and fair around the table.

"College ball is a lot different than high school. Way more competition, and I don't think he even went out for it here."

"The things you learn," Ava murmured, and I nodded. I never could have imagined our tall and thin friend hitting guys like this on the football field.

"How about you?" Phil broke apart a roll and ripped off one healthy chunk. "Do you play any sports?"

"Nope." I shook my head. "Not my thing. I like to watch, though."

That elicited hoots of male laughter, and I shook my

head. *Boys.*

"I mean, I like to watch football. And baseball. And even soccer. When I was a freshman, I covered the soccer team for the college paper."

"Really?" Marcus looked interested. "So you're like a writer?"

"Yeah, I'm like a journalist." I winked at him. "Or at least a journalism student. And I write for the school newspaper, too."

"Tell me something you've written recently. Maybe I read it. I check out the newspaper now and then." Kent looked at me, expectation in his eyes.

"Hmmm...well, a few weeks ago, I did a feature on how social media is changing our campus. It was part of a series."

"Hey, I think I read that." Phil nodded. "You said people were staying in their dorms more, not hanging at the SU so much. Right?"

"That was part of it." I laid down my fork and glanced across the table. Ava's eyes were tracking something—or someone behind me. She looked over at me and gave a barely perceptible nod. Liam was there.

I took a deep breath. Time to step up my game. But before I could say anything or try to get my flirt on, Marcus spoke.

"Yeah, social media. Like Facebook and shit, right? My roommate was telling me about this web thing, like, a page or something? A website? They want girls to go on there and bitch about how guys screwed them over." He shook his head. "Stupid crap. So all the girls are going to get themselves real worked up over, you know, like, life. It is what it is, man."

An odd mix of anger and interest ignited behind my eyes. "You think it's stupid? Have you read it?"

"Nah, and I'm not gonna, either. Waste of my time."

"Hey, dude." Phil caught his eye and shook his head. "Drop it."

"I'm just saying." Marcus leaned forward. "If guys did the same thing, talking about how girls treated us, they'd be moaning all over the place."

"Well, tell me about it." I pasted on a smile. "What has a girl ever done to you? Has she lied to you about who she was sleeping with, beside you? Pretended she loved you, then you found out she was with someone else?" I dropped the smile and pierced him with a stare. "Told you she was breaking up with you in front of a huge group of your friends?"

To my surprise, Marcus didn't back down. "Yeah. To all of that. You want to hear the down-and-dirty? I was in high school. First girl I ever—dated. She told me I was her first, and then she told me we were having a baby. I was like, man. I had this scholarship, I was going to play ball, but then I was having a baby? I went crazy, but I didn't let her down. I made plans, how we could get married, I could still come to school. Had it all worked out. So on Valentines' Day, I had a party, invited all our friends, and in front of everyone, I proposed. Down on one knee, the whole thing.

"And you know what she did? She laughed at me. Said the baby wasn't mine, I was her back-up plan, and the real daddy had stepped up. She was playing me to see how much I'd do for her, in case the other guy didn't man up. So, yeah. I know all about that. And you don't see me bitching on some Facebook page about it, either."

Marcus stood up, pushed back his chair and stalked away. I closed my eyes and swallowed hard, feeling small and stupid.

"Hey." Phil patted my arm. "Don't feel bad. You couldn't know."

"Maybe not, but I assumed. Sometimes..." I shook my head and stood up. "I need to go talk to him."

"Jules." Ava caught my arm. "Are you sure?" Her eyes darted to a table behind me.

"Yeah, I'm sure. I'll be back." I gave her a half-smile and wove through the tables, following the same path Marcus had taken.

He was still outside the dining hall, standing just beyond the doors. It was fully dark now, but the lights from the building glinted off his blond buzz cut. I took a deep breath and approached him.

"Hey, Marcus." I touched his arm. "I am really, really sorry. I didn't mean—no. I did. I just didn't think. I got all wrapped up in my own drama, and sometimes I forget I'm not the only one who's been hurt. And even that girls aren't the only victims out there."

"It's fine." He spoke through his teeth, and I knew it wasn't fine at all.

"It isn't. I mean, I don't know you. Not at all. But from what I saw tonight, I'd have to say, that girl was an idiot. I don't know why women act that way, any more than I know why guys do it. It just sucks."

"Yeah." He spared me a glance. "I know what Bailey did to you. I heard about it. You're right, it sucks." He set his mouth in a firm line. "That's why I told Giff I'd help tonight, you know? Because I know what it feels like. I thought, why

93

not help out someone who's been where I was?"

My stomach plummeted. "That makes me feel even worse. Here you and the other guys are doing me a favor, and I baited you. I'm sorry." I could only repeat the same words. Nothing I could say would take away what I'd done. Unless...

"Marcus, can I tell you something? Can you keep a secret?"

He cocked a brow at me, and I took that as assent. "The thing is, why I got all defensive about that website...it's my site. My idea. Well, mine and another girl's. It's part of an assignment for a class. And we were trying to let girls tell their stories about boyfriends behaving badly, but maybe our focus was too narrow."

Marcus nodded. "Okay."

"So maybe—could we tell your story on the site? Just as a look at the other side of the coin? And we'll widen our scope. I'll keep it all confidential, but we'll open up the site to boys' stories, too."

"I don't know. No one knows about me. I lived in South Carolina, and nobody else from my high school is here. Only the guys know." He pointed to the dining hall. "And only because I told them one night when I was wasted." He stretched back, looking up into the clear starry sky. "You'd make sure it couldn't come back to me? No one could figure it out?"

I nodded. "Absolutely. I'll change details. Make it general. But maybe it would help someone else to know he's not alone."

He was silent for a few minutes, and then finally he met my eyes. "All right. Let's do it. But I'm telling you, if anyone finds out it's me, I'm coming for you." He pointed one finger in my face, but the crinkling of his eyes took some of the heat of his words.

"You got it. I'm going back inside before I freeze to death. You coming?"

He shrugged. "Yeah, I still need dessert, right?"

We walked back into the dining hall, and as we cleared the food service section, Marcus slung one muscled arm around my shoulders and pulled me close. He leaned down to whisper into my ear.

"Bailey's over there, and his eyes are about bugging out his head. Want me to plant a wet one on you, right on the lips? Really give him something to wonder about?"

I giggled, raising my shoulder. Marcus' breath tickled my neck. "Thanks for the offer, but I think I've caused you enough angst for one night."

He moved his hand to close around my neck as we stopped at our table. "Aw, c'mon, sweetheart, just a little sugar."

With a twinkle in his eye, he leaned down and covered my mouth. It was more a sham kiss—his lips stayed closed—but it took me by surprise, and I imagined that from Liam's point of view, behind us, it looked a lot more involved than it was.

I gave Marcus a playful shove and dropped back into my seat. "Listen, you guys, thanks for doing this. I don't know how Giff gets people to help him out, but I do appreciate it. You're all really good sports."

Kent shrugged. "I have a little sister, and some dude hurt her like that, too. I want to mess up his face, but I can't, or I'd lose my place on the team. So this lets me feel like I'm doing something, you know?"

I smiled. "Yeah, I do. Thanks."

Phil laughed. "I just did it 'cause Giff makes me laugh. He's a good friend. Why the hell not? Just have dinner with two hot chicks?" He leered toward me. "Not really a hardship."

I covered his hand with mine. "Still, I'm grateful." I looked over to Ava. "Are you finished? Ready to go?"

"Hey, we eat with girls, we leave with them, too. C'mon, let's go." They all stood with us, and Kent grabbed for my hand, imprisoning it in his huge grip.

I didn't look toward where I assumed Liam was sitting; I just headed for the exit with my massive bodyguards.

Once we got back to our room, I pulled out my phone and opened my text messages.

Okay. Yes. What time tomorrow night?

Chapter Nine

Dr. Lamott, who taught my last class on Fridays, had a tendency to run late, and I was anxious to get to my car and head for work once he finally dismissed us. Focused on that goal, I almost didn't see my ex-boyfriend as he stepped into my path.

"Julia."

I careened to a halt, and the girl walking too close behind me smashed into my back. She favored me with a scowl and a muttered expletive.

Glancing up at Liam's face, I made to step around him, assuming he hadn't actually meant to make me almost trip. But he shot out an arm and stopped me.

"Julia, please. I just want to talk to you for a minute."

I blew out a breath. A cold front had moved in the night

97

before, ending our one day of near-spring, and the last thing I wanted to do was linger in the frigid air and shoot the bull with Liam Bailey.

"I'm late." I blurted out and then cringed. I wanted to be smooth and scornful, but instead I sounded ridiculous.

"For what? Your next class?" Liam dropped my arm and stuck his hands into the pockets of his coat.

"No, for work. I need to be at Dr. Fleming's house in twenty minutes. My last class ran long." I sidestepped off the path. "So I'll have to catch you later."

"Wait a second, I'll walk with you." He fell into step with me, and I rolled my eyes. All I had wanted out of this day was the chance to get through it and focus on my upcoming date with Jesse. I didn't plan to think about Liam all day. But here he was.

"What do you want, Liam?" This time I was able to affect disinterest and impatience, and I smiled a little in self-congratulation.

"I just wanted to talk to you. I know I don't have any right--"

"No, you don't. That's one thing we'll agree on."

His jaw tightened, and I recognized the expression of discomfort. *Good.*

"Julia, I'm worried about you. I haven't seen you around for a while, and then--"

"Oh, geez, let me think, why haven't you seen me around for a while? Seems like I used to see you quite a bit. Oh, that's right. You were my boyfriend. And you broke up with me. And didn't tell me. Until you had your arm down some slut's shirt, groping her in front of all of our friends. Yeah, it's coming back to me now."

Giff and I hadn't ever discussed how I was supposed to act if I came face-to-face with Liam, but it turned out that didn't matter. I was handling this fine on my own, and it was exhilarating.

Liam grabbed my arm and stopped, pulling me off the walkway. "Can't we get past this? I get it. I was a dick, you hate me."

I jerked my arm back. "First, don't use the past tense. From my point of view, you're still a dick. And get past it? Wow, Liam, I must have missed all your messages of apology. All the times you came by my room to explain? I guess I wasn't home."

He looked at the ground. "Fine, let it all out. Tell me how much I suck."

I stamped my foot in frustration. "God, Liam! You don't get it, and you never have. You're trying to make me sound unreasonable, but guess what, buddy? This one's all you. And yeah, you suck, but not even because you're a dick. It's because you're a coward. You weren't man enough to come to me and say what you wanted."

I turned and made it two steps before he caught my hand and pulled me back.

I looked up with narrowed eyes.

"Don't touch me. Ever." Anger boiled very near the surface.

Liam ignored me and snaked an arm around my back, over my bulky coat. "As I remember, that's not what you used to say. As a matter of fact, you used to beg me to--"

I shoved my elbow deep into his side, and Liam bent over with an oomph of air. I leaned just close enough for him to hear me.

"You're a pig, Liam, and I don't know what I ever saw in you."

I stalked up the rest of the path to the car, threw my bag into the passenger seat, climbed in and locked the doors, just in case Liam decided to follow me. I had to force myself to keep to the speed limit until I hit the open country roads. Then I let loose, rolling over hills and around curves.

My phone buzzed as I turned into the Flemings' driveway. I checked it once I was parked.

Are we still on for 6:15? I have class until 6, will just come right to dorm.

I smiled. That was exactly what I needed: a reminder that not all guys were Liam Bailey. I texted back quickly before I went into the house.

Yes, sounds good. See you then. Just got to your house.

Don't let the rugrat wear u out. Looking forward to tonight.

I hugged that little tidbit to me for the rest of the afternoon. He was looking forward to seeing me.

"Does the green look too much?"

I turned around from the mirror, holding a shirt in front of me. It was a deep green, with a low scoop neck and flowing sleeves. On the hanger it didn't look like much, but when I put it over my head, it clung and draped just right.

"Too much what?" Ava tilted her head, looking the outfit.

"You know, too much...like, too dressy for the movies."

"It's a date, Jules. You want to look pretty. Go for it."

I dropped the shirt over my head, pulled my hair out of the neck and studied my image again. Not bad. I'd made the effort to curl my usually-straight brown hair, and it looked good lying on the green of the shirt.

Next I debated between boots and my simple little black ballet flats and opted for the flats. There wasn't any snow on the ground, and they just looked better.

"Okay, I'm ready." I held out my arms and stood before Ava. "How do I look?"

"Breathtaking." She grinned. "Seriously, you look awesome. Go have a good time. Is Jesse coming up here?"

"He's coming to the dorm, but I think I'll go down and meet him."

She arched one eyebrow. "Really? What, are you ashamed of me?"

I laughed. "Of course not, silly. You can come down with me if you want. I just don't want him to have to brave the Friday night freshmen." The girls in our dorm tended toward craziness on weekends, and sometimes it just wasn't pretty.

"I think I'll pass. If I go out there, someone who's having a crisis will find me and need nurturing. If I stay in here, there's a better chance the crisis will pass before she can track me down."

"Hope springs eternal." I shrugged into my coat. "Well, wish me luck."

"You don't need luck. Just relax and enjoy yourself." Ava gave me a quick hug. "And text me at some point, so I know he hasn't taken you to the woods to be his love slave."

"Please!" I rolled my eyes and opened the door, jumping

back in surprise when I saw Liam standing on the other side.

"We need a peephole in this door so we don't open it to just anyone," I muttered to Ava. She looked back at me with wide eyes.

I attempted to step around Liam. "Excuse me, I need to leave."

"Where are you going?" His voice was tinged with surprise, which just pissed me off even more.

"Out."

"Where?"

"None of your business."

"She has a date." We both turned to stare at Ava. She stood in the middle of the room, arms folded over her chest.

"That's right." I smiled and shimmied past Liam. "And I don't want to keep him waiting."

"Which one of your new men are you seeing tonight? Do you know what everyone is saying about you? Or don't you care?"

Without turning around, I bit my lip, counted to ten under my breath and took a deep breath before I spoke.

"I thought I made it pretty clear this afternoon, I'm not your business anymore, Liam. If I want to bang the whole football team, I will. So, good night, and don't let the door hit you in the ass on the way out."

"But I wanted to talk with you. This afternoon--"

"Should have told you everything you wanted to know. Leave me alone, Liam. Please."

"How about this, Liam." Ava had moved closer to the door, but the look of determination on her face hadn't faded. "You tell me what you have to say to Jules, and I'll decide if it's worth her time. If it is, you can talk to her later, when she's ready." Over his shoulder, she caught my eye and mouthed *Go.*

I practically sprinted down the hall and the steps, running smack into Jesse as he came through the double doors into the lobby.

He caught my arms to steady me, smiling down. "You really do know how to make an entrance."

"Sorry. I was trying to save you from the throngs of freshman girls who hang out in the hallways on Friday nights here."

The dimples popped out, and I sighed. It was an automatic response, one I hoped he didn't notice.

"I appreciate that. As I remember, freshman girls can be a little intense."

"You don't know the half of it. My roommate Ava is a saint. She has so much patience with them."

Jesse stepped back a little, looking at me. "I like your shirt. It makes your eyes look really green. Since you didn't get mad at me for saying it the other day, I'll chance it again. You're very pretty."

I laughed. "Any girl who gets mad at you for saying that is crazy. I promise I never will." I bit my lip. That sounded a little too much. Like I expected him to say it often.

But Jesse didn't seem bothered. He held out a hand to me. "Are you ready to go?"

I hesitated only a moment before nodding and slipping my hand into his. "Very."

It was bitterly cold, and I shivered when the air hit me. Jesse dropped my hand and put his arm over my shoulders, drawing me closer to his body heat.

"C'mon, my truck is just up here."

I had never noticed what Jesse drove since he usually parked in the garage at his dad's house. I was a little surprised when he led me to an old white Ford pick-up and unlocked the passenger door manually.

"Sorry, my sweetheart is a no-frills gal." He patted the side of the truck.

"I love it." I climbed inside and scanned the vinyl seats, the basic dashboard and plastic floor mats. It was a stark contrast to Liam's Beemer, which almost drove itself. I liked that Jesse opened my door for me; Liam had always just clicked the unlock button from his key fob and expected me to get in by myself.

I leaned over and pulled the lock up on the driver's door. Jesse opened it and slid in next to me.

"Thanks." He slammed the door and turned the key, fiddling with the heat buttons and directing the vents my way.

"It'll warm up in a minute." He rubbed his ungloved hands up and down his thighs over worn jeans. My eyes tracked the movement, and my mouth went dry.

"Hey, Julia." Jesse reached across the bench seat, touched the side of my face. I smiled, and he let his fingers move down to my chin. The brilliant blue of his eyes fastened on my mouth before he met my gaze.

"I know this is going to sound corny, and like it's a line or something. But it's really not. Which also sounds like a line. When you get to know me better, you're going to find out I'm not that smooth. But I've been thinking about tonight all week. And if I have to wait through the movie, and then dinner and then whatever else we might do, I'm not going to be able to relax and enjoy myself."

"Wait to do what?" I whispered the words, mesmerized.

"Didn't I say it? Hmm." He moved over, his hand going under my hair to cradle my head.

"No, you didn't say." His face was so close to mine that I couldn't focus on his eyes anymore. I closed mine in surrender.

"To kiss you." His lips were a breath away from my own, and my heart stuttered. "Is it all right? May I kiss you?"

My tongue darted out instinctively, wetting my lips. Jesse drew in a sharp breath.

"Yes. Please." I barely breathed the words before he moved the last fraction of an inch closer and covered my mouth.

He didn't mess around with a tentative first kiss. His lips were open, and I was startled to realize the moan I heard came from my own throat. His tongue teased the inside of my mouth and then stroked against mine. At some point, my hands had moved of their own accord to wrap around his neck. My fingers itched to plunge into those brown curls, but I was still wearing my gloves.

Jesse broke away just enough to take a breath, leaning his forehead against mine. He dropped his hands to my back and then to my waist, all on top of my coat.

"Damn." He pulled me closer, trailing kisses along my jaw to my ear. "I hate cold weather."

I giggled, shivering again as his breath tickled my neck. "Why?"

"Too many layers." He dropped one last kiss on the tip of my nose, holding my face between his two hands. "But probably a good thing now, or we would totally miss the movie."

I smiled. "What movie?"

"Ah, see, you're not a good influence!" He moved back over behind the steering wheel and reached for his seat belt. "If we didn't have the movie, I would want to take you back to my house, and...well, I'm having trouble remembering why that wouldn't be a good idea, but it wouldn't."

I buckled my own belt. "Let's just say, we can't let down Joss Whedon by not going to see the movie. Right?"

He cast me a sidelong look. "It's a reason. Not a good one, but it's a reason. So, now let's do what normal people do on a date. Did you have a good week?"

I cast my mind back over the past few days and inwardly cringed. There wasn't much I could tell Jesse without going into details I couldn't share yet. Telling him, on our first date, that I was in the middle of trying to get revenge on my ex just didn't seem like a good idea.

Although...there wasn't any reason I couldn't tell him about the blog. As long as he didn't give the information to anyone else, it was just a class project.

"Yeah, it was busy but good. I'm working on something for my social media seminar, and getting it off the ground took a little while." I gave him a general overview of what we were doing, focusing more on the research element than anything personal.

"Huh." He shifted into a third gear as we turned off campus. "That's...interesting. Are you worried people are going to get upset about their exes outing them on the Internet?"

"We don't use any names, and we change crucial details." I paused, thinking of Marcus. "To be honest, we planned to focus only on women scorned. But then I talked to someone, a guy, who'd had a bad experience with a girlfriend, so we're equal opportunity now."

"Sounds fair. I've heard horror stories on both sides."

I glanced at Jesse. "So do you have any horror stories of your own? Not for publication, just...curious."

He chuckled, swinging the truck down a quiet street. "You think I'm going to tell you?" He shook his head. "Okay. It was a very painful episode in my life, so you have to promise you won't laugh."

I put my hand over my heart. "You have my word."

"I was totally in love with a girl...her name was Andrea. I gave her my everything, all my attention, showered her with gifts, and then she threw me over for my best friend. In a very public way."

My mouth dropped. "Oh, Jesse, I'm sorry. I didn't mean to pry—and why on earth do you think I would laugh at that?"

"Maybe not that, but when I tell you how far it had gotten between us..." He looked at me from beneath his eyelashes. "I gave her my animal cookies."

For just a minute, I was completely confused and must have looked it, because Jesse doubled over in laughter as he pulled the truck alongside a curb.

"Animal cookies—how old were you?"

Jesse held up a hand. He was laughing too hard to answer at first. "We were six. First grade."

"Oh!" I swatted him and then crossed my arms over my chest, feigning annoyance. "Here I thought you were telling me about the great love of your life."

He shook his head. "Aw, c'mon. That was heartbreaking. She took everything I gave her, and then when she was team captain for kick ball, she picked my best friend first, instead of me. I saw the writing on the wall."

I shook my head, rolling my eyes. Jesse released his seat belt and leaned over, giving me one quick kiss. "Are you too mad at me to enjoy the movie?"

I raised my eyebrows. "Do you think I could let your mockery of heartache get between me and Joss? No, sir."

"Okay, then." He was out of the truck and around to my side before I could reach for the door latch. He took my hand firmly in his to help me climb out and then kept it, lacing our fingers together as he bought our tickets.

The theatre was a quaint old building, all red velvet seats and curtains, shining brass railings and plaster bric-a-brac. Jesse led me about half-way to the huge screen before we chose a row. The cavernous room was nearly empty, with just a few other patrons scattered here and there.

"This is beautiful," I whispered once we were seated.

"Isn't it? I read about it online. It's got a great history. I love old movie houses. It's a shame most of them are being torn down."

I nodded. "My grandmother took me to see *Gone With The Wind* at a theatre like this. It was amazing. That was how those old movies were meant to be seen."

"Yeah." Jesse was quiet for a minute. Our joined hands lay on the wooden armrest between us, and he tightened his grip. "I really didn't mean to make fun of your project before. I think it's cool that you're trying to help people, even if I don't totally get it. I haven't had anything like that happen to me. Most of the people I've dated have been friends, and when we stopped dating, we stayed friends. No drama."

The lights dimmed, and the opening strains of the

theatre promo music sounded. Jesse tilted his head closer to me.

"What about you? Have you had your heart broken?"

I bit the side of my mouth. I wanted to be honest, but I also wasn't ready to tell the sordid story of Liam's birthday party.

I turned my head to whisper into his ear. "Ask me again some time."

He met my eyes and after a moment, nodded. The coming attractions trailers began, and I focused on the screen.

Chapter Ten

"If there were ever any doubt about it, let it be wiped away. Joss Whedon is a freaking genius."

Back in the truck, the heater was just beginning to warm the air as Jesse pulled away from the curb.

"True. You liked it then?"

"I really did. Well, come on. Shakespeare. You just don't get any better. And then Joss putting his own spin on it. It was amazing."

"You know my favorite part?" Jesse smiled at me sidelong.

"Hmm. Probably a scene with Amy Acker, right?"

"Nope. Although she was pretty hot. No, it was watching you mouth all the lines along with the actors."

"I so did not do that. Did I? Oh my God, how embarrassing. I'm sorry." I covered my face.

"Don't be! It was cute." Jesse snagged my hand again. "So are you hungry?"

"Famished."

"Good, because there's this diner I want to take you to. Open all night. It's totally south Jersey and all chrome and plastic. It's got a juke box, too."

"Sounds like heaven. How did you find it?"

He lifted a shoulder. "I was out driving around the other night, and there it was. I thought it would be a good place for a post-movie meal."

I smiled. *He had been thinking of me?* I held his hand just a little tighter, and he squeezed mine in response.

The diner was a small square of silver on the corner of two streets. An older woman with bluish hair led us to a booth and tossed two laminated menus on the table.

"What looks good?" Jesse scanned the specials and glanced up at me.

"Waffles." I closed my menu and pushed it away. "Waffles with strawberries and whipped cream. And a chocolate malted milkshake."

"Well, that was quick and definitive."

"I am very specific in my diner food preferences. How about you? What are you getting?"

He narrowed his eyes. "A chili cheesedog with curly fries—and I'll have a milkshake, too." He lay down his menu on top of mine.

The waitress sauntered over to take our order. "Do you want chopped onions on that dog?" she asked Jesse.

His eyes skittered to mine, with a question, and I felt my face grow warm.

"Nope, no onions." He raised one eyebrow, smirking,

and the waitress sighed deeply before she shuffled away.

Jesse reached across the table and took my hands in his. "I'm glad we decided to do this. To go out, I mean. Thanks for saying yes."

"Thanks for asking me." I squeezed his fingers. "So I told you about my week. How was yours?"

He shrugged. "Not bad. I'm still getting used to everything. You know, living with Dad and Sarah and the kiddo. I don't think they know what to do with me sometimes."

I smiled. "I think they're glad you're there. Sarah always says nice things about you. It might just take time."

"Probably. It's just..." He made a face. "I've lived with my mom and sister since my parents got divorced. I visited Dad, but living here is a whole different ballgame, at least in my mom's eyes. She's not happy, even though she knows it was the best option for me. And when my mother is upset, my sister is mad, too. So I'm dealing with both of them."

"Ugh." I shook my head. "I can't imagine. That sucks."

"It really does. This week, Mom called wanting to hear all about everything. School, the house, the whole nine. I didn't talk about Dad and Sarah, because I didn't want to make waves, but then she complained that I was keeping things from her. And when I did tell her, she picked apart everything. I said Sarah cooked a good dinner, and she said I must love finally living with a family where there's a good cook." He heaved out a sigh. "It was like being stuck in one of those perpetual loops. That's why I ended up out here driving around for hours. Dad overheard me talking to my mother, and he got mad at her. I just got in my truck and drove."

"I'm sorry." I turned my hands so that I could entwine our fingers again. "They've been apart for a while, haven't they? You'd think by this time, they'd have learned to deal with everything gracefully."

"Right? Mom was okay about me moving here. I'm twenty-two years old, for God's sake. I lived at SUNY for four years without either of them." Jesse frowned, and then shook his head again, as though to clear it.

"Anyway. That's how my week went. Classes are good. I talked to my advisor, and I can get an internship for the summer, working at the clinic."

"What exactly will you be doing? I remember we had an SLP at my school when I was growing up, though we just called her the speech teacher. The kids who had lisps or whatever had to go. I was jealous that they got out of class."

Jesse laughed, and there were the dimples. I swallowed hard and focused on what he was saying.

"I'll be working with people of all ages, from little kids just starting to talk to people who've had strokes or brain injuries. We diagnose and recommend courses of therapy."

The waitress appeared again, this time with all of our food. We were quiet as she plunked the dishes down in front of us. Jesse thanked her, and I offered a big smile, but she just grunted as she walked away.

I dug into my waffle with gusto while Jesse attempted to tackle the messy chilidog with the help of a huge pile of napkins.

I swallowed a bite. "You know, I never even thought of speech pathologists working with anyone other than kids. That's pretty cool."

Jesse poked his straw into the thick milkshake, chewing

a bite of hotdog. "In my undergrad internship, I worked at a nursing home. I got to see them do swallow tests, that kind of thing. I think that might be where I want to work eventually."

"It must be nice to know what you want to do." I nabbed a strawberry and dragged it through the whipped cream, then brought it to my lips and licked off the cream before biting into the berry. When I looked up at Jesse again, his eyes were fastened on my lips and his mouth hung slightly open.

"Are you trying to kill me?" I could barely hear his words, and I was confused until I realized the end of the strawberry was still in my fingers. My lips curved into a slow smile as I leaned forward.

"Kill you? Why, whatever do you mean?" Never dropping my gaze, I nabbed another strawberry and drew circles in the cream. I brought it to my lips and bit.

Jesse closed his eyes and let out his breath, leaning back against the booth. A moment later, he raised his hand to get our waitress's attention.

"Can we get our check, please?"

"Did you see how our waitress looked at us? Like she thought we were going off to do something nefarious."

We were both laughing as we returned to the truck. Jesse started it up and turned in his seat to look at me.

"So...I guess it's time for me to take you back to the dorm."

I smiled. "Unless you have something else up your

sleeve. It's almost eleven. You're welcome to come up and hang out with Ava and me in our room, but it *is* just a room. There's no, um, expectation of privacy."

Jesse nodded. "I understand. I lived with a roommate for four years." He popped the clutch and put the truck into gear, pulling out onto the silent street. "I'd say we could go back to my place, watch a movie or something. Or even just talk. But I'm not sure it's a good idea."

I bit back the sting of disappointment. "You don't?"

Jesse must have heard the hurt in my voice. "Julia, it's not that I don't want to. I do really, really want to take you home with me. But this is our first date. It's been awesome. I had an amazing time tonight. I don't want to rush anything. And if I took you to my apartment, even though I'd want to be a gentleman, I'm pretty sure being alone with you would trump all those good intentions."

I nodded. "I had a really good time, too."

We were silent as the truck ambled along the back roads. Jesse held my hand when he wasn't shifting. As we pulled onto campus, he finally spoke again.

"Julia, can I ask you something?"

His tone was serious, and I frowned. "Of course."

"You're not...seeing anyone, are you? I know you said you'd just ended a relationship, but—there's no one else?"

I opened my mouth to answer. Once upon a time, that would have been a simple reply. Now...I thought about Jack Duncan and about the trio of football players I'd eaten dinner with the night before. I wasn't seeing them; it was all part of the game. But to someone from the outside, it might not look that way.

"No, I'm not dating anyone." I played with the button

on my coat. "Like I told you before, you could hear about it around campus, so I might as well tell you. The relationship I was in last year was with a guy who...well, he's a big deal on the track team, and his dad is in politics. Everyone knows him. Liam, I mean. And his dad, too. It was pretty serious. At least I thought it was serious. I guess he didn't. And the ending was messy."

"Okay." Jesse coasted the truck into the gravel lot adjacent to my dorm. He parked and put on the brake before he turned to me. He laid his arm over the back of the bench seat and regarded me steadily in the dim light of the street lamps and the glowing dashboard.

"Was that relationship last year ...are you over it? Over him? Or am I the rebound guy?"

I was so surprised my mouth dropped open. I shook my head. "Oh, no, no. No rebound. No, I'm totally over him. He was—it was--" I tried to think how Ava had described my relationship with Liam.

"I think it was just something that happened. We started dating, but we really didn't have anything in common. Or not much, at least." I thought of all those months. "We fought a lot. And not in a passionate way." My face heated as I struggled to explain it. "I am pretty sure I annoyed the crap out of him sometimes. And I never felt like I was important to him. Sometimes I felt like his parents liked me more than he did. So yes, it was kind of hurtful, but not devastating." I turned to look Jesse squarely in the eyes. "He didn't break my heart. Because he never had my heart."

Jesse was quiet, his eyes on the seat between us. When he glanced up at me, a smile hovered around his lips.

"That's good to know. I didn't want to be weird about

that. Or jump the gun on anything. But I like you, Julia. You're fun, and funny, and smart, and damn pretty." He reached his fingers to brush the strands of my hair that lay over my coat collar. "I didn't want to go any further into something that didn't have potential."

"So do you think we do have potential?" I slid toward him, just a fraction of an inch.

The smile grew, and damn, there were those dimples. Jesse moved closer. "I'm pretty sure the answer is yes, but maybe we should test the waters, just to make sure. I mean, what if we don't really have any chemistry?"

"That's true," I agreed. "It would be tragic to find that out too late."

"Mmm hmmm. C'mere." His voice had thickened, and when he slipped his hands under my coat, I wondered if he could feel the thunder of my heart. I lifted my head just in time for Jesse to crush his mouth to mine.

The jolt was insane. It was like a line ran straight from our joined lips down my middle, and fire licked along that path. Jesse's hands slid around to my back, pressing me closer. I had just enough presence of mind to pull off my gloves and drop them onto the seat behind him before the kiss consumed me again. I plunged my fingers into the soft curls on the back of his head.

"Mmmm." I hummed in appreciation, and Jesse backed up a little to look at me in question.

"What was that?" He kissed down my neck, and I let my head loll back to give him better access.

"I love your hair." I couldn't believe I'd said it out loud, but Jesse only laughed.

"Really? I always hated it. Other boys made fun of me

for having curly hair when we were in grade school." He found the hollow at the base of my throat and circled his tongue there. I sighed.

Jesse's hands were at my sides now, moving up and down in time with the rhythm of his kisses. I held his head in place as he plundered my mouth with lazy intensity. He wasn't rushing, but there was no doubt about his passion.

I eased back, thinking to lean against the door. Instead, I fell onto the seat, with Jesse on top of me. In the process, I hit my head on the door handle.

"Ouch." I freed one hand to rub the sort spot. "Jesse, I really like your truck. A lot. But it's not made for...umm...this."

He sighed and braced his weight onto his hands on either side of me. "I think if we got creative, you'd be surprised. I've never put it to the test, you understand, but I'm having ideas now."

He sat up and offered me a hand, helping me back onto my seat.

"Is your head all right?" He probed my hair with careful fingers. "Do you think you have a concussion? I'd be willing to stay up with you all night. You know, to make sure you don't fall asleep. People with head trauma shouldn't go to sleep."

I laughed. "Sorry, as tempting as that is, I don't think I have a concussion."

"Well, it's on your head. Literally."

I rolled my eyes and pulled my coat back into place. "I guess I better go inside."

"Are you sure? I am really re-thinking that whole first-date-good-intentions thing. I have a perfectly good guest house just a few miles away, with a very comfortable…sofa."

"I'll bet you do. Maybe I can take a rain check?"

Jesse gave an exaggerated sigh. "Of course." He laid back his head, eyes closed. "I think I should walk you to the door. I need the cold air anyway."

I reached across and touched the curls over his ears. "I really did have a good time tonight."

"Me, too." He ran the back of his fingers over my cheek. "So we know we have Joss in common, and I know you have a Shakespeare fetish."

"It's not a fetish." I scowled at him. "It's an appreciation."

"Yeah, whatever. So what else do you like to do?"

I cast my eyes up, thinking. "I like to read. I like to write. And cook. Oh, I love to watch sports. Football especially. And I like the beach, too."

"That's some pretty random stuff. And the beach is way too cold this time of year. But the football. I can work with football. What are you doing for the Super Bowl? I was thinking of inviting some guys from the SLP grad program over to watch it. I have a decent TV in the apartment. Want to come, too?"

I pretended to consider. "Hmmm. Are you just inviting me so I'll cook for you?"

Jesse's eyes lit up. "You'll cook for us? Hot damn. Okay, I'll give you a menu, you give me a shopping list. It'll be fun."

Laughing, I shook my head. "How did I get suckered into that? All right, I'll cook. Let me think about what I want to make. We'll work out the menu together, okay?"

"That would be perfect." He took my hand again. "I

want to see you again. This weekend I can't, because my sister is coming down tomorrow and it's going to be big drama. It always is with her. Believe me, I'd much rather be with you." He paused, and I could tell he was thinking, even as his thumb made lazy circles on the back of my hand. "Weeknights are hard. I have evening classes on Tuesdays and Thursdays. Would next weekend work? Maybe on Sunday, you could come over. I'll get take out and we can watch a movie. What do you think?"

"I think it sounds great." I hesitated. "Did you tell your dad and Sarah that we were going out tonight? Are they going to be okay with it? With me being over there next weekend, I mean? I don't want things to be weird between us, and I really don't want to lose my job."

"I told Sarah I was going to see you tonight. She was glad, said she was hoping I'd make some friends around campus. She likes you. They both do." Jesse kissed the top of my head. "Try not to worry about it."

"I'll try. I better go inside."

Jesse opened his door and began to climb out. "What's this...?" He picked up something off the ground and held them out to me. "Your gloves?"

I put them back on and held my hands to my face as he slammed his door and came around to my side.

"Brrrr! I am so over winter!" I slid off the seat, but Jesse stood in my way, his arms trapping me as he lowered his head to mine.

"It just occurred to me that I haven't kissed you standing up yet," he said, as he did just that. Just the barest touch of lips, as I stood feeling completely vulnerable, and at the same time, perfectly safe within the cage of his arms. It was so sweet, so light. I swallowed hard and lowered my face so he couldn't see how much he affected me.

"Let's get you inside," Jesse whispered. He took my hand, and we dashed to the lobby doors.

He insisted on walking me all the way upstairs. Technically, boys weren't supposed to be beyond the downstairs lobby after eleven on week nights and midnight on Fridays and Saturdays. It was just after that now, but since I roomed with the resident advisor, I wasn't too worried about her ratting me out.

We snuck past several groups of girls, watching a movie in the lounge, hanging in the hallways to talk or popping popcorn in the small dorm kitchen. I saw more than one set of curious eyes follow us. One pair belonged to the freshman girl Liam had brought to his birthday party. I wondered if he was still seeing her, or if he'd thrown her away, too.

Ava was still awake when we got to my room. She was lying on her bed, and I noticed that her eyes were a little puffy. She put on a bright face when she saw Jesse with me, and I introduced them again.

"Do you want to sit down? Have something to drink before you head out again?" Ava offered Jesse. "Our entire bar and kitchen is at your disposal."

He smiled, and when his dimples appeared, I saw Ava's eyes widen. I smothered a giggle.

"Thanks, but I better get home. I'm helping out with the little bro tomorrow morning so my dad and step-mom can have a breakfast date. I hear he's an early riser, so I should probably grab some sleep while I can." He caught my eye. "Walk me out?"

He waved to Ava as we stepped into the hallway. "Why

did you walk me all the way to my door if I'm walking you back out? Doesn't that defeat the purpose?"

Jesse held me by the upper arms and drew me closer as we stood just beyond the door to my room.

"You don't have to walk me downstairs or outside. I just wanted one more goodnight kiss before I head out into the cold, cold world."

"I think I can manage that." I stood on my toes to touch his lips. Jesse tightened his grip on me and kept me in place while he deepened the kiss. Leaning against his body, I could feel every ridge, every muscle against the length of my body. I never wanted to move.

"Good night, Julia." He released me, keeping one hand on my shoulder until he was certain I was steady. "I'll call you tomorrow?"

"Yes. Please." I smiled up at him. "But not when you get up with Des. I'm sleeping in."

Feigning dismay, Jesse put his hand to his chest. "What kind of nanny are you, that you can't offer me emotional support while I take care of your beloved charge?"

"The kind who needs her sleep when she's not on the clock. And he's your brother, so that trumps nanny." I stepped back to the door, laying my hand on the knob. "Thank you, Jesse, for a beautiful night."

"You're very welcome." He started to walk down the hall and then turned back to look at me. "Hey, Julia? You're still very pretty."

Laughing, I watched until he disappeared down the stairwell. I could hear him whistling as he went.

I opened the door and floated back into my room. Ava still sat on her bed. She had a faraway expression on her face, but she smiled and looked up at me when I closed the door.

"Well? Come on, tell all. I want details. How was the movie? Did you go to dinner? Did he kiss you? And oh, God, Jules, those dimples!"

I leaned against the door and dropped my head back.

"Oh, Ave...I think I'm in trouble."

Chapter Eleven

Pounding. Someone was pounding on my head. And there was moaning. I had been having such a wonderful sweet dream, and the person who was pounding on my head was annoying.

"Jules, it's someone at the door." Ava pulled the pillow up and over her head. "Make them stop."

I stumbled from bed and made sure I was decent in my shorts and t-shirt. Opening the door a crack, I saw Giff, standing in the hallway with a donut box, a tray of coffee and a smile that was far too bright for so early in the morning.

"Oh, my God, Gifford! Go away. It's the middle of the fucking night!" I left the door opened and fell back in the direction of my bed. Early morning hours tended to bring out my profanity.

"Well, rise and shine, sleeping beauties! Look what I've

brought you. Donuts and fresh coffee from Beans. Mmmm. Doesn't it smell good?"

Ava moaned again and let loose with something unintelligible. I opened one eye and glared at Giff.

"What time is it and why in the name of all holiness are you here at this hour?"

"It's after eight, and I am here because the perfect opportunity has just opened up for you today. I thought I was out of favors and ideas, but then something, ummm, popped up last night. I was going to call you, but one thing led to another, and I kind of forgot. But here I am this morning, bearing gifts." He pointed to the coffee again.

I turned over and buried my face in my pillow. Ava and I had stayed up much too late talking about Jesse, and the situation with Giff, and every other complicated, screwed-up element in my life. We'd counted on being able to sleep in. I had even turned off my phone in case Jesse thought it would be cute to call me when he got up with Desmond this morning.

But clearly nothing stopped Giff when he was on a mission. I felt my bed dip and knew he had sat down next to me. I wondered if I didn't move, if he'd eventually go away.

It didn't seem likely. I shifted, turning my head so I could breath.

"Okay, early bird who gets the worm. Tell me why you're here. But hand me one of those coffees, first."

Giff jumped up to retrieve the cup and pass it over to me. I plumped up my pillows and settled back to try and stay awake.

"I was at a party last night, and I got chatting with someone I used to know a few years ago. We lost touch."

Giff studied a tiny thread on his jeans, and I wondered if this someone was an old boyfriend. Giff, who wanted to know everything about everyone else, was very circumspect about his own personal life.

"So it turns out he's a manager for the wrestling team, and they have a meet today. And his brother is single and in town. Used to be on the team, so he's coming to the meet. Jeff says he'll definitely be game to meet you there, hang out, make it look flirty. As a favor to his little brother. You know the drill."

I felt ill. "Giff, please tell me why I'm doing this? How is Liam even going to know I'm there?"

He smiled. "I'm dragging my roommate to the wrestling match because this cute guy I met last night is going to be there."

I groaned. "Giff, he never goes with you anywhere to meet guys. You really think he'll do that?"

"I know he will, I already talked to him. He'll go with me because I've been giving him the guilts so bad about what he did to you. He's trying to be a better person."

I snorted. "Yeah, I bet. Did he tell you what happened yesterday?"

Giff frowned. "He said he'd seen you. But he was vague. And when he got back to our room last night, something was wrong. He wouldn't tell me what."

I glanced at Ava. "He came by here when I was on my way...out. So he talked to Ava."

She was still buried beneath her comforter and pillow but lifted her head just enough that I could see one open eye. "Told you. He said he's worried you're hanging around with the wrong guys." The eye closed and the head dropped.

"He stopped me on the way to work yesterday afternoon, too, and when I wouldn't chat, he started playing the martyr card. No explanation, no apology, just woe-is-me crap."

Giff smiled big. "Jules, that's awesome. You've got him thinking about you. See, didn't I tell you it would work?"

I set down the coffee. That sick feeling was back. "Yeah, you told me. You're the man."

"Yes, I am. Which is why you're going to get your sweet ass out of bed and head for the gym. Today might be the tipping point. You could be back in Liam's loving arms tonight." He paused and shot me a wolfish grin. "Which could work out for me, too, depending on how things go with Jeff and me at the meet."

I shook my head at him. "What time do I have to be there?"

"Eleven. Oh, Jeff's brother is Dean. He's got red hair, and he'll be looking for you. I sent Jeff a picture of you." Giff stood up. "Make sure Princess Pea gets her coffee, okay? I want full credit for bringing breakfast. See you in a little while."

He was out the door before I could answer. Ava lifted her head again.

"Quick, lock it before anyone else comes in. Good God, have people never heard of Saturday? The morning when you don't wake up your friends?"

I jumped out of bed and turned the bolt on the door. Passing the box of donuts, I snagged a chocolate frosted on the way back to bed. My stomach was still rolling, but chocolate never hurt anything or anyone.

We both dozed another hour or so before I dragged

myself upright. Ava was beginning to show signs of life as I came back into the room after my shower.

"Was Giff really here this morning, or did I have a very detailed nightmare?" Her voice was still muffled.

"He was here. Good news is he brought coffee and donuts. Bad news is he set me up with someone else."

She struggled to a sitting position. "Was there something about wrestling? I thought that had to be a dream."

"It wasn't, sadly. I'm going to a meet this morning."

"Oh, Jules." Ava pried the plastic lid off her coffee cup, took an experimental sip and made a face. "It's cold, can you zap it for me?"

I tugged on my jeans. "Yeah, just a second." I took the cup and stuck in the microwave for a minute.

"Do you want me to come with you?" She gave me the pitiful poor-Ava look.

"No, I'm not that mean. But I was thinking after Giff left. I'm putting my foot down. This is it. I'm done. Liam isn't jealous about me hanging out with guys. You said last night he only wanted to warn me away from hanging with them, right?"

Ava jumped out of bed and opened the microwave to retrieve her coffee. She tested it and then blew across the top, all of while she avoided looking at me.

"Ave?" I pulled a red henley over my head. "Are you okay?"

"Of course." She attempted a smile. "Why wouldn't I be?"

"I don't know, you got a funny look on your face. Did Liam say something else last night? When I got home, your

eyes almost looked like you'd been crying. You can tell me
if Liam was a jerk. I really don't care."

"No, I told you everything. He was trying to find out
why you're seeing all those guys, but he says it's just because
he doesn't want you getting hurt. I asked him why it mattered
to him, when he hadn't done a very good job of not hurting
you himself. He said he felt like it would be his fault if you
were doing it just to get back at him."

I flushed. "I'd say his ego was a little inflated if he
wasn't actually on to us. So he's not interested in me because
I'm unattainable again, he's worried that my broken heart is
making me a little too attainable. To other guys, at least.
Lovely."

Ava turned away from me. "Where are the donuts?"

"Over on my desk. Seriously, Ave, are you okay? You
look...weird."

"I'm fine, I'm just a little tired still. I think I'll crawl
back under the covers and go to sleep for a while." She
snagged a donut and napkin from the box.

"All right. If you're sure." I ran a brush through my hair
and caught it up into a high ponytail. My boots were lost in
the bottom of my closet, so it took me a few minutes to dig
them out and get my coat. By the time I was ready to leave,
Ava's eyes were closed, and her even breathing told me she
asleep. Or doing a darn good impression of it.

I left the room as quietly as possible, still wondering
what was going with my roommate.

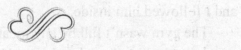

I didn't spend very much time near the sports complex on campus. I'd had a yoga class there during freshman year; it filled the physical education requirement without forcing me into a competitive sport. I'd been to a few basketball games when Liam made me go with him, but since the track and field facility was on the other side of the campus, we spent more time there than in the gym.

There was more than one event going on that morning, so it took me a little while to figure out where the wrestling meet was taking place. I was just about to open the door when I heard someone calling my name.

"Julia?" A man about my height, stocky with red hair, walked toward me. He smiled as he came near.

"You *are* Julia, right? I'm Dean Lester." He held out a hand. "Good to meet you."

"Yes, I'm Julia. Hi, Dean." I forced a smile I was far from feeling.

"My brother tells me we have a job to do today."

"Oh, really? And just what did he tell you? I like to know what my friend Giff is saying."

"Just that I'm supposed to keep you company, make it look good. Like we maybe have something going."

"Mmm." I nodded. "Okay. Well, don't worry too much about that. Let's just have a good time, and maybe you can even explain to me how these matches work. I am totally clueless about wrestling."

"You've come to the right place. I've been wrestling since I was five years old." Dean opened the swinging door, and I followed him inside.

The gym wasn't full by any means, but there were more people on the bleachers than I would have expected for a cold

Saturday morning. I was aware right away that Liam and Giff sat midway up in the center section.

"Let's sit over here." Dean guided me with his hand on my lower back. We climbed up a few rows on the right side and sat down. I left a judicious amount of space between us and looked down at the mats.

"So what's going on down there?" I propped my elbows on my knees and leaned my chin on one hand.

"That's Jennings, there. He's about to wrestle that dude from Cramer."

I made a face. "I don't like their outfits. They look like giant baby suits."

"They're called singlets."

"Yeah, well, they don't leave much to the imagination, do they?"

"They're designed to keep opponents from grabbing onto clothing during matches."

"Hmm. Okay, I guess that make sense. What about the thingie on their heads?"

"Headgear. It's protective. Are you anti-all sports or just wrestling?"

"Hey, that's not fair. I'm not anti-any sports. I actually am quite the sports fan. Just not this. I mean, check out at how they look down there, compared to eleven men on a hundred yards of vivid green. Not dressed in funny-looking onesies."

Dean shook his head. "Football. Really? A bunch of guys trying to move pigskin down the field ten yards at a time? Don't get me wrong, I dig a game now and then, but it doesn't even approach the artistry of what you're going to see here."

He pointed to the mat, and I focused on two men who paced just outside the ring that was painted on the foam. At the signal from someone I assumed was the referee, they both approached center and dropped on their haunches to a crouch. They moved in wary half-steps from that position. The man in the red onesie—I mean, singlet—grabbed the other guy by the head. In turn he grasped his opponents' arms, and they went around and around.

"So far it doesn't look much different than two boys fighting it out on the playground." I kept my voice low; I didn't want to offend any of the fans around us, who apparently saw more than I did if their yelling was any indication.

"Just watch." Dean's eyes never left the match, and they were bright with attention. I stifled a sigh and turned my attention back to the men on the mat.

"Oh, now wait a minute. What is this?" The ref stopped the match and said something I couldn't hear. The blue wrestler dropped to his hands and knees, and red wrestler came up behind him, in some kind of backwards hug. It looked downright...pornographic.

"He's going to—oh, dude! Did you see that escape?" Blue guy had executed a sort of fancy twist and gotten to his feet, knocking red guy away in the process.

"Yeah, that was something." There was more of the head grabbing, some arm and shoulder grasps, and then a whistle blew.

Dean let out a breath and leaned back, rolling his shoulders as though he'd been in on the match.

"What's happening?" Both wrestlers had moved to side, were conferring with other men and chugging water.

"End of the first period. If there's no decisive win or disqualification in the first three minutes, there's a second period."

"And then that's it?" If he heard the hope in my voice, so be it. Wasn't like I really cared what he thought of me, anyway.

"Well, depends. If nothing happens in the second period—that's two minutes—then there's a third. And then if it's still tied, there's overtime. That's sudden victory, tiebreaker, second overtime round--"

"You have got to be kidding me." The wrestlers were returning to the mat as I watched. "What do they have to do to win? And which one there is from Birch, 'cause I'll start cheering now, if it ends this whole thing sooner."

Dean seemed not to notice my lack of enthusiasm. He kept his eyes on the match as he began.

"There's point scoring, and you can win that way. It's called a technical fall. But you can also win by fall, by decision, by default..."

He kept talking, but I tuned out the words. I loved to learn anything new, but I was fairly certain understanding wrestling was not going to enhance my life in any way.

As I pretended to be absorbed in his explanations, I let my eyes drift to the next set of bleachers. Giff was leaning back on the empty bench behind him, his blond hair artfully mussed. He wasn't so much watching the wrestling as he was the side lines—I supposed they were called that—where a guy who bore a passing resemblance to Dean was studying a clipboard.

Aha, the brother. I couldn't get a good look at him, but he seemed to have a similar build to Dean. His hair wasn't red, though; it was jet black, and he raked his hands though it as he flipped over papers and spoke to wrestlers on the bench.

I glanced back, hoping to catch Giff's eye and give him a wink, but it was Liam who was looking my way instead.

His dark brows were drawn together, and his jaw was tight. I shrugged and turned back to the wrestlers just as a cheer went up.

"Did you see that? He just won the match. Awesome." Dean's enthusiasm didn't spread my way, but I did my best to clap as though I cared.

"So he won...it's over now?" Yes, that was hopefulness spiking in my voice.

"His match is over, but now other wrestlers will compete."

"How many?" Visions of my entire Saturday consumed by this farce danced behind my eyes.

"Two more. In this weight class, I mean. And then there's nine other classes."

"*Nine* other classes?" I dropped my head into my hands. "So you basically hang here all day watching this?"

Dean spared me a quick glance. "Well, yeah. I came back just to see this meet."

"That's right." I turned again to see if Giff were paying attention. He wasn't; he had instead taken advantage of the momentary break in the action to snag a few minutes with Dean's brother. And Liam was nowhere to be seen. I assumed he had fulfilled his roommate duty and blown this joint. I was about to do the same.

"So, listen, Dean, this was fun. I really appreciate you teaching me a little about wrestling. I feel much more informed."

He grinned. "Sure, anytime. There's a lot more to see and learn. The next match is about to begin."

"Yeah, I see. But unfortunately I have a few things I need to get done today. So I'm going to have to head back to my dorm. Thanks again. It was...interesting."

Dean seemed to look at me a little more closely than he had since we entered the gym. "You know, I'm down here quite a bit. I'm work for a financial services company, and I travel. Maybe some time I could call you up, take you to dinner?"

Oh, dear God, the last thing I needed was another male in my life right now.

Aloud I said, "Thanks. That's nice of you. Let's see what happens, but I'm kind of, um, seeing someone else right now. Sort of. I mean, it's new."

He nodded. "I get it. Is it the guy you're trying to make jealous? 'Cause I'm not an expert or anything, but that doesn't seem like a good way to start off."

"No. That's someone else. He's—well, it's complicated."

"Sounds like it is. Well, it was nice meeting you, anyway." He smiled as the next match got underway.

I climbed down the bleachers and headed toward the exit. The hallways beyond the gym were quiet, and with tremendous relief, I pushed open the doors to fresh cold air and freedom. I stood for just a moment, glad that was over.

"Julia."

"Oh, my God!" I jumped as Liam stepped from around a column. "You scared the crap out of me. What are you doing?"

"Waiting for you."

I swallowed my nerves. "I've never had a stalker before. It's creepy. You should give it up."

"I'm not stalking you." Liam's lips were drawn together and his eyes dark.

"Then why are you skulking behind columns outside the gym, waiting for me?"

"I wanted to talk to you."

I rolled my eyes. "You've spent more time wanting to talk to me in the last few days than you did the entire time we were dating. Doesn't that strike you as odd?"

He ignored me and grabbed my arm. "Can we go somewhere and sit down? It's cold out here."

"Liam, I don't have time for that. I'm sorry."

"Why? Got another date waiting for you?" His tone was suggestive and snide at the same time, and I held back a wince. This was what I'd been working toward, wasn't it? Getting Liam's attention, making him want me again?

"Not this morning." I tossed it back to him. "I'm going to hang out and study with Ava."

It was Liam's turn to react as though I'd smacked him. His frown deepened, and I saw his throat work as he swallowed.

"I just want a few minutes. Look, come sit in my car. It's parked right over there. I promise, I only want to talk."

I threw up my hands. "Fine. Whatever. But five minutes, tops. Then I need to get back to my room."

He nodded and turned toward the parking lot. I followed him to where the black BMW was parked and climbed in when he clicked the button, aware again of the differences between my ex-boyfriend and Jesse.

He didn't say anything as he turned the key and upped the heat. When he did shift to face me, I was surprised by the conflict in his eyes.

"Julia, I wanted to talk to you about all these guys you've been...with. What's going on?"

I raised one eyebrow. "What do you think is going on, Liam? And why is it any of your business?"

"Because I think it's my fault. I think I broke your heart, and now you're trying to get attention wherever you can, but you're not thinking about this right, Julia. You--"

"Whoa." I held up one hand. "Stop right there. You know, just when I think I've reached the bottom level of your jerkiness, you show me that you're even more of a dick than I thought. You broke my heart? Really?"

He looked away, uncomfortable. "Yeah, I think I did. I mean, I did what I needed to do, but I can see that it must have been hard on you."

"My God, Liam. You are incredible. You *needed* to do that? You *needed* to humiliate me in front of our friends, and even some strangers? Explain that to me, please."

He lifted one shoulder. "It was time. Things had gotten too serious between us. I was ready to move on."

"So you're ready to move on. Fine. I get that. A normal guy would tell his girlfriend that. He would man up enough to actually break up with her. You are so damaged, Liam. I really don't know why I wasted ten months of my life on you."

"You weren't complaining at the time. I think you liked being Liam Bailey's girlfriend. Which is why I had to do what I did. At the party. If I had talked to you, there would have been drama and tears and shit. This way, it was done.

Like a surgical strike."

I reached for the door handle. "You know what, Liam, we're done here. I don't have anything to say to you, and I definitely don't want to hear any more from you."

"Wait." He grabbed my shoulder.

I glared. "Get your hand off me unless you want your arm back without it."

He sighed. "Why does everything have to be so complicated, Julia? I just had something to say, and you made this into a big deal."

"So say it."

"Okay." He took a breath and looked out the window beyond me. "You don't need to chase after all those guys. If you're missing me, we can work something out. You know, nothing serious. Like friends with benefits."

I'd heard of people being choked with rage, but I'd never had it happen. I did now.

"Are you fucking kidding me?" I hissed the words, too angry to yell. "You think that's why I'm...God, Liam. Your balls are bigger than even I thought. And when were we ever friends? Tell me that. Benefits we had, but friendship, not so much."

"Hey, hey, I'm just trying to help you out here--"

"Yeah, *help me out*. I'll just bet. How selfless you are, Liam. It just brings a tear to the eye. Umm, let me think. No. I'd prefer the self-service plan to your benefits any day."

"Nice, Julia."

"The truth hurts. You're worried you broke my heart? Here's some news for you. You never had it to break." I had said the same thing to Jesse the night before, and I was struck anew at how true it really was.

"That's bullshit. You're just still pissed about my birthday, and I get it, but come on. Try to be a grown up about this."

"It's not bullshit, it's the truth. Think about when we first started dating. Tell me about that. Who was after who?"

He shifted in the driver's seat again, looking decidedly ill at ease. "I don't remember."

"Liar." I pointed a finger at his chest. "It was you. You stopped me outside biology that day and asked me to go to some frat party with you. I said no. So then two days later, you asked me to some movie thing on the campus green. I said no."

"Yeah, you played hard to get."

"I wasn't playing, Liam. I didn't want to go out with you. I didn't like you. I thought you were pretty much what I think about you now."

He frowned at me. "Then why did you finally say yes?"

I sighed. "Because...you seemed so subdued and quiet when you asked me the third time, to go out to dinner. And you hit me on a bad day. Someone else I really liked had just started dating a girl I knew. I thought, why not go out with someone else?"

He rubbed his hands across the steering wheel. "So I was convenient."

"Maybe. Wasn't I convenient for you? And we had a good time that night, remember? I came home and told Ava maybe you weren't that bad."

"Please, Julia, don't try to flatter me. You know what? None of that matters. Why we started dating, why we stopped, it doesn't matter. It's the here and now I'm talking about. You're hanging around with all these guys, and people are starting to talk. I mean, Jack Duncan? Seriously."

I gritted my teeth. "Jack is a decent guy. You wouldn't know about that. And I'm fairly certain I said before...it's none of your business. You were done with us, right? Move on, Liam. I have."

He smirked, that maddening half-smile that always went right up my spine. "It's my business because you were mine first. Or should I say because I was your first?" He lifted a shoulder. "Let me put it to you this way, Julia. Letting you screw around with these other guys would be like me going to a gourmet restaurant and then giving my leftovers to the bums on the street."

The fury was back, full force. I grabbed the latch and swung out my door. Scrambling out wasn't exactly as satisfying as storming off, but it was all I had. I leaned back into the car for a moment.

"Liam, you're not worth my energy. Stay away from me. You might have been my first, but let me tell you, you're not the best. You're not even in the top ten."

I slammed the door full force, knowing how much he hated that, and wished that he and his precious car would go off the nearest cliff. In fact, I spent the first part of my walk back to the dorm picturing how glorious that would be.

The second part of the walk, I spent plotting.

Ava was up and in sweats when I came into the room. She sat on the floor with books spread all around, a pencil behind her ear, and her laptop to the side.

"Hey..." She trailed off, her forehead crinkled. "What's wrong?"

"Liam Bailey is what's wrong. He's very, very wrong." I tore off my coat and tossed it up on hook, not caring if it caught or not.

"So I take it he was there? At the match?"

"It's called a meet, and yes." I dropped to the edge of my bed. "I spent over an hour learning more about wrestling than I ever wanted to know. And then when I finally escaped, made it outside, *he* was waiting for me. Turns out he's come up with a great idea. A really selfless plan designed to help me out. He's willing to sleep with me, just out the goodness of his heart. Isn't that big of him?"

Ava's already-ivory complexion seemed to go a few shades lighter. Her eyes got huge, and her mouth dropped a little.

"He what?" She almost whispered the words.

"Yep, you heard me right. Sex without any of the annoying strings attached. That's what he's offering me." I gripped the sheets. "I just want to scream. I haven't been this mad since right after his birthday party."

"I don't blame you." Ava hugged her knees up to her chest. "That's...that's just horrible."

"You know, the sad part is that I had started to second-guess everything. I was planning to back off the whole revenge plan. Not now. Now, I'm upping the ante."

"What are you going to do?"

"No more playing around with Giff's plans. I'm going to tell him what his precious best friend said to me. And then I'm going to write out the whole sordid story, from the time he asked me out, all about the birthday party and then about today's mess. And I'm naming names."

"Jules, really? Is that going to solve anything? And what about Jesse?"

I cringed a little. "I know. I thought about him right

away. But God, Ave, Liam deserves some kind of payback for everything he's done to me. This is totally separate from Jesse and me."

"Can you keep it that way? Don't you think he's going to find out and maybe not be happy?"

I blew out a breath, pushing my hair away from my face. "I'll burn that bridge when I get to it."

Chapter Twelve

Jesse called me right after dinner. Ava and I had decided to eat in, mostly because I didn't want to chance seeing anyone I knew at the dining hall or the student union food court when I was still so mad, and Ava said she wasn't feeling well. And come to think of it, she looked pretty rough.

We were sitting on the floor, various containers of take-out food opened around us, and *You've Got Mail* on TV, when my phone buzzed.

"Hey." Even his voice made me smile. I must have looked pretty goofy, since Ava rolled her eyes, even as she tried to hide a grin of her own.

"Hey, yourself. So you survived Des duty?"

"Oh, yeah. I bribed him to stay in bed a little longer with Spiderman cartoons and chocolate chip cookies. I laid down next to him and slept."

"So you probably got crumbs in your bed and a hyper kid."

"Definitely, but an extra hour of sleep was totally worth it. How was your day?"

"Ehh." I stood and moved into the hallway so Ava could hear the movie in peace. "It was okay." I hesitated a moment and then plunged ahead. "Actually, it kind of sucked. I had a run-in with my ex-boyfriend, and I spent the rest of the day trying to work off my mad."

"Ah. Gotcha." I heard him suck in a breath. "Okay, no, not really. I don't know what you mean. So you want to tell me, or should I mind my own business?"

I leaned against the wall and slid down to the floor. Damn, but this guy was like the polar opposite of Liam. *Thank God.*

"He was a pig. Let's leave it at that. He was insulting and rude, which he does very well. But you know what, talking to you right now makes me feel better than I have all day."

"Good." I could practically hear those dimples pop out. "I feel like I should offer to, I don't know, beat him up or something. Like, defend your honor?"

"That's sweet, but I defended it just fine on my own. If it comes down to it, I'll let you know and you can totally take a swing at him, okay?"

"It's a deal." There was enough warm humor in his voice to make me melt.

"Are you having a good time with your sister?"

I heard his sigh. "I should say yes. Alison's not a bad person, but sometimes she sucks the life out of me, you know? She makes Sarah nervous, because she's ready to jump on her for anything she says or does, and then Dad gets mad."

"Does she at least like Des?"

"Yeah, when she lets herself. It's like she's afraid loving him means she's not supporting my mom."

"I'm sorry you have to deal with all that."

"Yeah, well, she'll be gone tomorrow afternoon, and then I just have to do all the homework I should have been doing all weekend."

"Speaking of which..." I stood up. "I better get back to this blog post I'm putting together. And Ava's got the movie on pause. I can't keep Tom Hanks hanging on any longer."

"Fine, ditch me for Tom. Meanwhile, I'm on my own."

I laughed. "Use your imagination."

"I hope you don't mind that in my imagination, my sister is gone and you're sitting in my lap?"

"Not at all."

"So which one next?" Ava held up two DVDs. "More Meg goodness with *Sleepless in Seattle*, or be daring and move on to Katherine Heigl with *The Ugly Truth*?"

"Decisions, decisions. Okay, let's try Heigl and Butler. I could use some sassy fun."

"Great, but if we go that direction, I need chocolate."

"Don't tell me the chocolate drawer is empty!" I clapped my hand over my heart in mock horror. "How could we let that happen?"

"All right, smart ass, laugh it up, but it's your turn to make a food run. I'm thinking Crunch bars and maybe some peanut butter cups."

I sighed, deeply and with great meaning. "Fine. I'll go out in the dark and cold to get your fix. Just remember this next time I need sour cream potato chips."

"Yeah, whatever. Make it snappy."

I tossed Ava a not-so-friendly gesture, shoved my feet into the furry slipper shoes that were good for this kind of on-campus errand and put on my coat. The halls were quiet for a change. The girls were either out already for the evening or hunkered down with books and movies, like Ava and me. I ran into a few of them in pajamas or sweats on their way to friends' rooms, but no one stopped me for information or advice, which was a nice change. Maybe our little freshmen were finally growing up.

The student union was only a few minutes' walk from our dormitory, and the sidewalk was well-lit. I kept my head down and scurried along. I wasn't worried about running into Liam; he'd be out for the evening by this point.

Almost no one was in the snack shop at the SU. The cashier looked bored as she leafed through a magazine and talked on the phone.

I stood before the candy rack, trying to decide what I felt like eating. I found Ava's requests and had just picked out a chocolate bar with almonds for myself when two guys walked in the door.

"Jules?" Giff laid a hand on my shoulder. "I thought that was you. What are you doing, trolling for chocolate?"

I turned, smiling up at him. "Hey. Yeah, it's a movie night. Gotta have our snacks." I glanced behind him, where a familiar dark-haired man stood at the drink cooler.

Leaning toward Giff, I lowered my voice. "So wrestling worked out for you?"

He flushed a little, and then grinned. "Yeah, you might say. Dean said you hung for a little while, but then you bailed."

I shook my head. "Only so much wrestling a girl can handle. I mean, of the spectator sport-kind."

He nodded. "Yeah, I guess. But maybe next week we can—"

"Giff." I took his hand, squeezed it. "You're a wonderful friend, to both Liam and me. But your roommate and I had a heart-to-heart this morning after the meet, and I can tell you what you and I were planning isn't going to work. I wish I didn't have to say it, but he's a bigger jerk than even I thought. I don't want him back. I'm sorry you went to all that trouble."

Giff frowned. "I knew something went down. Liam wasn't there when I got back to our room. He'd gone running, and he'd gone hard. He was snarly and nasty when I asked what was up. And then he showered and went out tonight. Didn't say where."

I shrugged. "Whatever. He can do anything or anyone he likes, it really doesn't matter to me. But you do matter. So can we still be friends, even though you live with a dick?"

"Honey, we're all dicks. And of course, I'm always your friend. You can't shake me loose that easy." He turned a little as the other guy approached. "Jeff, this is my friend Julia. Julia, this is Dean's brother."

I offered my hand, smiling. "Your brother's a good sport. Tell him I said so." I held up my candy. "Now I'm taking my chocolate and getting back to Gerard Butler. You two..." I winked at them. "Behave yourselves. Catch you later, Giff."

It felt good to have everything out in the open with Gifford. One less snarl in my life. I hurried back to my room and dumped the candy onto Ava's lap.

"Here you are, my lady. Are we queued up and ready?"

"You bet. Mmmm, thanks." She tore open a wrapper, bit into the Crunch and pointed to the screen as the opening titles appeared. "Ever notice that Gerard is a little bit of jerk in this movie?"

I laughed as I settled back into movie-watching mode. "I have it on good authority that honey, they're all dicks."

Chapter Thirteen

It snowed again the next week, just enough to make it a pain in the neck to get around campus. I hated having to wear my boots to class and sit there for an hour, feeling like the abominable snow woman about to melt into a puddle in the over-heated classrooms.

Just to add to my irritation, Ava was acting strange. If there was one thing I could count on in my life, it was her steady presence in our room, always studying or writing papers. Unless she was going out with me to eat or leading a study group, she was at her desk or in bed with books.

When I came back to our room on Tuesday and found it empty, I didn't worry, figuring she had gotten held up after class. But when I glanced up at the clock later and realized it was after six, I reached for my phone to text her.

She didn't reply. I was just about to call her when the

door opened.

"Oh, my God, you had me worried. Where've you been? And what's wrong?"

She was flushed and frowning. "I'm sorry. Impromptu study group after class and I figured it wouldn't take that long, but then it did."

"Ave, what happened?" She was practically shaking as she shrugged off her coat and hung it up.

"Nothing happened. I got a C on the quiz in cog psych. It was stupid, and I'm mad at myself."

"Are you sure that's all?" I knew Ava was uptight about her grades and hated getting anything under an A, but I'd never seen her this upset about a quiz.

"Yeah. Listen, I'm going to skip going to dinner tonight. Can you bring me something back from the SU? I need to get to work. I'm really behind."

"Sure." I pulled on my boots and coat. "Anything else I can do?"

She shook her head, but her eyes didn't meet mine. "No, thanks. I just need a little time to think. To study."

But it was more than that. For the rest of week, it felt as though she was avoiding me. We ate together, but more often than not, it was a rushed meal before she hurried back to the dorm to do homework. She was quiet and looked so awful that I wondered if she might be sick. At the same time, she seemed to be out more than I was used to, telling me she had a meeting or was tutoring. It was so completely unlike her that I was uneasy.

The bright points in the week were when I got to see Jesse. He was too busy with classes and school work to go out at night, but we managed a few minutes here and there when he came home in the afternoons.

"I'm going to get fat." He patted his flat stomach after I'd served him homemade pizza leftover from Desmond's lunch. "And spoiled."

I shook my head. "Don't get used to it, buddy. I'm just luring you in with good food."

"And then you'll have your way with me?" He grabbed my hand and pulled me onto his lap as I passed his seat.

"Jesse, Desmond--"

"Is sound asleep upstairs. I can hear him breathing through the monitor. And Dad and Sarah won't be home for another couple of hours." He wiggled his eyebrows at me, trying to be suggestive but only coming across as comical as a cartoon villain. "I've got you all to myself."

"Oh, woe is me." I wriggled in his lap, smiling when I felt his response and heard the sharp intake of breath. I linked my hands behind his head. "Whatever will I do?"

He lowered his mouth to mine. "Give in. There's nothing else to do..."

"If I must." I managed to get out the words before he covered my lips, his tongue making insistent forays against mine. A thrill of desire shot through me, and I was lost...at least until I heard Desmond waking up.

Our afternoon encounters kept me going, but I was looking forward to the weekend, to spending some time with just the two of us, alone. Jesse had promised to go to a basketball game on Friday night with his dad, and on Saturday, I had a conference for journalism majors in Philadelphia. I didn't get back to Birch until after seven.

Ava wasn't home, but before I could wonder about it, my phone rang. I smiled when I saw Jesse's number.

"Hey. Perfect timing, I just got back."

"That's me, perfect. How was the conference?"

"Oh, fine. All the people I'm going to be competing with for jobs in about a year, gathered in one place to hear how those positions are disappearing. It was a feel-good fest."

"Lots of sexy Tom Brokaw-wannabes?"

I laughed. "Maybe. You jealous?"

"Nah, Tom Brokaw was never my type. So are we still on for tomorrow? I was thinking mid-afternoon, a couple of DVDs, and I'll get food from someplace."

"That sounds amazing. You know what, though, don't get food. I'll go to the store on my way over, and I'll make us something. I mean, if that sounds okay. If you'd rather have take-out, that's cool, too."

"No, oh, God, no. I'd rather have real food, but I didn't want you to feel like you have to cook. I mean, before next weekend, with the Super Bowl."

"I can handle it. Being in the kitchen is therapeutic. Anything you feel like especially?"

"Anything at all. I am the non-pickiest eater you've ever met, I promise."

"Fabulous. I can be really creative then. Did you know you actually can buy cow brains at the grocery store now?" I struggled to keep the giggle out of my voice.

"Uhh, I hope you're joking. I'm not picky, but I'm not that adventurous either."

"Totally kidding. I promise. What time do you want me?"

He dropped his voice a little. "I want you now."

A thrill of electricity ran down my middle. "Oh." I spoke on a rush of breath.

"But I guess tomorrow about three works, if that's okay with you."

"I can do that. What are you doing now?"

"A research paper on dysphasia in middle grade children. It's riveting."

I laughed. "I bet. I have big plans: working on the blog and doing an outline for a paper. Maybe watching a movie."

"Which one? Just so I know not to get it for us tomorrow."

"Ah, probably a chick flick. *Sleepless in Seattle.* I think you're safe. Unless you've got a thing for Meg Ryan. About fifteen years ago."

"She's hot, no question, but I don't think any of her movies were on my short list for tomorrow."

"Okay. You surprise me about the movies, I'll surprise you about the food."

"That's a plan. I guess I better get back to work here, so I can enjoy you tomorrow." He paused. "I mean, enjoy being with you. Sorry, that came out wrong."

"I don't know, it sounded okay to me."

He laughed, low and intimate. "Do you know what I'd be doing if I were with you right now?"

My heart thumped. "No...what?"

His voice was a husky whisper. "I'd touch your face. Just lightly, just my finger tips. And then I'd lean...closer...and a little closer...and I'd brush my lips across yours. Run kisses down your neck, to that little hollow dip in your throat, where I can feel your pulse. My hands would be low on your back, just above your hips, pressing you to me."

"Oh...my...God." I closed my eyes and tried to breathe. "You're killing me."

"This is payback for the strawberry from the other night. At the diner, remember?"

"Ah. I need to remember to add those to my shopping list, huh?"

"Only if they come with whipped cream."

"The best berries always do." I drew in one long breath. "Okay. Back to work for you. And for me...on to Meg Ryan. See you tomorrow."

"Can't wait. Oh, and Julia?"

"Yeah?"

"You're very pretty. 'Night."

I grinned and hugged the phone to me, like a girl on her first date.

When I was college shopping, my parents were particularly enthusiastic about Birch because of the freshman single-sex dorms and because of the number of churches right off campus. Not that we were a super-religious family, but services on Sunday mornings were part of my weekly routine growing up. So I compromised by committing to going to church once a month at least.

I hadn't been at all since coming back from winter break, so knowing I'd need a distraction from obsessing about my date with Jesse that afternoon, I decided to bite the bullet and go.

"Hey, Ave, want to go to church?" I nudged her gently on my way to the shower. Although Ava was Catholic and I was Anglican, sometimes we went together. The traditions were just about the same, anyway.

"Hmmm?" She opened one sleepy eye. "Oh. Nah. I went yesterday."

"You did not."

She rolled over the pulled the blanket tighter to her shoulder. "Did so. While I was out. Confession and noon mass at St. Anthony's. Go 'way and let me sleep."

"Okay." I went into the bathroom, frowning. Ava was more devout than me, I knew that. But still, it was unusual for her to go to confession, and even odder for her to go to mass without mentioning it to me.

I put on one of the few dresses I'd brought to school, pairing it with boots and my long coat. The church was close enough to our side of campus that it was just as easy to walk as it was to move the car, so I made sure to pull on gloves and a scarf as well.

It was cold out, definitely, but maybe not quite as biting as the day before. The sun shone down on my back, and I enjoyed the quiet of the early Sunday morning sidewalks. Telling Giff to cool it on the win-Liam-back plan last week had taken a huge weight off my shoulders, and I walked with a lighter step. Aside from the other complications of the week, it had been a relief not to have to hang out with guys I didn't know. I'd still overheard a few rumors about how I was going off the deep end after getting dumped by the great Liam Bailey, but that would die down soon. Getting past Liam once and for all—or at least heading in that direction-- felt good.

St. Thomas's was a small stone church just beyond Birch's gates. I smiled at the elderly lady in her long camel coat and small matching hat climbing the steps ahead of me.

Two little boys burst out the wooden doors, chasing each other and nearly knocking into the woman before their mom grabbed them by the collars.

I held the door, and hat lady flashed me a thank-you smile. "It's lovely to see young people at church."

"Thanks. It's good to be here." We both moved down the aisle toward pews.

I breathed in the undercurrent of incense as I sat in the back of the church, going through the motions that were so familiar. Stand, sit, kneel. The sermon was about forgiveness and grace, and a twinge of guilt struck me.

I knew, as I sat there considering it rationally, that writing about Liam and what he'd done to me wasn't going to make me feel better. At best, it could backfire and ruin my friendship with Giff. At worst...I squirmed a little. What would Jesse think? I hadn't gone into details with him about Liam, let alone tell him about our public break up.

But I was almost stuck now. The blog was moving along, and every day, Kristen and I got more emails and messages with stories. If I didn't tell my own story, would I be wimping out? Letting down the people who were opening up to us? Or was that just my own justification for doing something, anything, that would embarrass Liam as much as he'd humiliated me?

The piano began to play again, and I realized the service was ending. I slipped out the back and headed to campus, still no closer to an answer that made me feel better.

The grocery store where I stopped on the way to Jesse's was crowded with people trying to stock up before the work week began. I flew through, tossing penne, tomatoes and cream into my cart, grabbing a wedge of Parmesan, a half-pound of prosciutto and some fresh basil—along with some very pricey fresh strawberries-before I paid and trundled it all out to the car.

It was weird to be driving to the Flemings' house on a Sunday, when I wasn't going to spend time with Desmond. My anticipation of being with Jesse again just about balanced the nerves over the possibility of seeing Sarah and Danny. What would they think?

The house was quiet; I didn't see any movement through the kitchen windows as I pulled back into the driveway. A porch light burned in the winter afternoon dimness over the back door, but other than that, everything was dark.

The guest house was attached to the garage, its door just a few steps from the main house. I parked to the side of the driveway as I usually did, leaving plenty of room for other cars to get around me.

I climbed out and slung the groceries over my shoulder just as I heard a door open. Jesse jogged over and reached for the canvas bag.

"Hey." He smiled, his eyes meeting mine. "Any more in there, or is this it?"

"Just the bread." I leaned back into the backseat and pulled out the long loaf of Italian.

"Cool." He waited until I stepped beyond the door and slammed it closed. Then, his smile deepening, he moved closer, trapping me between him and my car.

"Hi." He didn't whisper, but his voice was still low

enough to give shivers that had nothing to do with the dropping temperatures.

"Hi." I licked my lips without thinking about it, and Jesse's gaze dropped to them. He leaned toward me, dropping his mouth over mine, just a light welcome kiss. He brought one hand to the side of my face and amped up the intensity, touching my lips with the tip of his tongue until I opened them.

"Jesse." I half-moaned his name and broke away to glance at the house. "I don't want Des to look out here and ask what we're doing."

He laughed, not moving an inch. "They're not home. Went to spend the day at Sarah's parents. Won't be back until after dinner."

I arched my neck back to look at him. "Really?"

"Really." He kissed me once more and ran his hand down to take mine. "Let's go inside before you freeze to death."

I had never been inside the guest house. The front door opened into a small sitting area, with a tiny kitchen on the side. Beyond that I could see an open door that I assumed led into the bedroom and bath.

Everything was simple and neat, from the beige carpet to the blue valances over mini-blinds that covered the few windows. It was warm, cozy and inviting.

Jesse dropped the bag onto the kitchen counter and came back over to take my coat.

"I don't know what goes in the fridge and what doesn't, so go ahead and make yourself at home." He tossed my coat over a chair while I emptied the bag.

"I hope you like Italian." I shelved the cream and cheese

in the mostly-empty refrigerator. "This is some of my favorite comfort food, but it's also slightly trendy."

"I love Italian. What are you making?" He came up behind me and slid his arms around my waist. My heart stuttered a little, and I bit back a sigh.

"Penne a la vodka. Have you had it?"

"Mmmhmm." He nuzzled my neck. "It's one of my favorites."

I stilled and swallowed hard. Jesse's hands were low on my stomach, near my hips. I could feel all of him along my back, solid and so tempting. And so clearly wanting me.

He raised one hand to move my hair out of the way and kissed up the column of my neck. I sagged against him, closing my eyes.

"I'm sorry." He murmured the words into my ear, and I wriggled, shivering. "I know. You just got here, and I'm groping you."

"Did you hear me complain?" I turned in his arms and ran my hands up his neck, behind his head.

"No." He rubbed my back. "But I don't want you to feel like that's why I invited you over here. I just can't seem to not touch you."

I leveraged myself up to kiss him. "Again, no protests here."

"Mmmm." Jesse turned and lifted me onto the counter. "Are you sure about that? Because encouraging me is only going to make me worse." He stepped between my knees and ran his hands up my thighs before pulling me into another deep kiss.

His mouth was incredible. He coaxed my lips apart and then swept his tongue inside, tangling with mine. I clung to his neck, my fingers playing with the soft curls there.

Jesse trailed his hands up my sides, brushing his thumbs under my breasts. Teasing, just barely touching me, making my heart pound and my body yearn. I sucked in a breath, and he moved back just a little.

"Sorry." He kissed down the side of my neck again, his voice not quite steady. "If we don't cool down a little, we're not going to get to the movie. Or dinner. Or maybe even class tomorrow."

"Remind me where that's a bad thing?"

He laughed. "You're not helping. Here we go." He boosted me off the counter and sighed. "Movie wonderfulness awaits us over here."

I sat on the sofa, and Jesse picked up a remote before he joined me, sitting close enough that our legs touched. He clicked on the television and draped an arm over the back of the couch behind me.

"So what did you decide on?" I shifted a little closer.

"A stroke of genius. We both love Joss, and we need an action movie. Well, I needed an action movie. So..." He hit the play button. "*The Avengers*."

I grinned. "One of my favorites. You couldn't have done any better."

"Huh." He fast-forwarded through the previews. "Do I rock or what? But seriously, you're okay with this one?"

"Umm, Chris Hemsworth, Robert Downey, Jr. and Jeremy Renner? Are you kidding?"

Jesse shook his head. "Nice. Way to make me feel secure in my manliness. So later when I kiss you, you're going to be imagining I'm Thor? Or Hawkeye?"

"Thor? Really?" I raised one eyebrow in mock

skepticism.

"Okay, I see how it is." He settled back as the movie began. "Don't forget Scarlett Johansson is in this, too. Black Widow is smokin'."

I snuggled down as he curved his arm around me. "I'm very secure. It wasn't Scarlett you had hot on the counter five minutes ago."

He lifted my chin with one finger, turning my eyes toward him. "I had you hot?"

"Shhh, I like the beginning."

"How badass was Iron Man in that movie?" I dug through a drawer in the kitchen. "Hey, do you have measuring spoons?"

Jesse shrugged. "I don't know. Maybe? Sarah put the bare essentials in here. I don't cook, so who knows?"

I gave up. "I'll make do. Can you grab me the cream from the fridge?"

"That I can do." Jesse pushed off the counter where he'd been leaning to watch me cook and retrieve the container. He set it down next the stove. "So you really think Ironman is the leader of the Avengers?"

I nodded. "No question. I mean, Hulk, he's got the brute strength, but not so much with the reasoning skills, right? Captain America is hot in a clean-cut retro way, but he's still getting up to speed on the twenty-first century stuff. Thor's just a visitor. He's not from earth. And Hawkeye and Black Widow...well, they have potential, but not the whole package.

Yet." I eyeballed what I hoped was a tablespoon of tomato paste and added it to the pan.

"You've obviously given this a lot of thought." Jesse stood with his arms crossed on his chest.

I grinned at him. "I never thought I was a geek. I don't love comic books or anything, but I have to admit, I'm a sucker for superhero movies."

"What about Spiderman?"

I raised my eyebrows. "Oh, yeah."

"Which one? New or old?"

I checked the pasta. The penne was still a little too al dente. "New. I don't have anything against Toby, but Andrew Garfield and Emma Stone?" I fanned myself. "Yeah. Definite chemistry." I cut off a chunk of Parmesan cheese. "I guess there's no chance you have a grater?"

Jesse smiled. "That I do have. The one meal I can make is nachos, and I like to shred my own cheese." He dug into a drawer and handed me the flat grater.

"Thanks. But just so we're clear, nachos are not a meal. They're a snack." I grated the cheese over the sauce.

"Oh, come on, they have all the major food groups." He ticked them off on his fingers. "You got your corn in the chips, that's vegetables. You got your cheese, that's dairy. Toss on some chili from the can, that's protein, right? Perfect meal."

I rolled my eyes. "Whatever. Do you have a colander?" At his look of complete ignorance, I elaborated. "You know. To drain the pasta. Like a bowl with little holes in it?"

"Pretty sure I don't."

"Okay, then, do me a favor. I'm going to pour the water out into the sink, and I need you to hold the lid on the pot so the penne stays in. Got that?"

"I think I can manage it." He stepped closer to me, and I breathed in his scent—a slight undertone of cologne, his shampoo and something that was uniquely Jesse. I bit my lip and focused on not burning either of us with the steaming water.

He watched me add the pasta to the saucepan, toss them together and lift the whole thing from the stove.

"I never knew cooking could be such a turn-on to me."

I shook my head at him, smiling. "Jesse, what isn't a turn-on to you?"

He considered. "About you, nothing. At least nothing I've seen so far."

"Well, then, get ready..." I dropped my voice into a seductive whisper. "Dinner is served."

We sat at the counter, and I scooped out servings onto the white plates I'd found in the cabinet. Jesse speared some penne and took a bite.

"Oh, my God." He closed his eyes. "I totally renounce nachos as a meal. This is incredible. I'm sorry, I think I'm going to have to keep you here to cook for me forever."

"Hey." I bumped my shoulder against his as I ate. "What is this, 1950? If you want to keep me in the kitchen, you need to offer some incentive."

"I provided the movie. What else do you want?"

I raised one eyebrow. "Use your imagination. Again."

Jesse was quiet as he ate, and I wondered if I'd said something wrong. Before I could get up the courage to ask, he spoke.

"I do use my imagination. Probably too much." He flashed me a quick smile. "But I wanted to tell you, this isn't normal for me. I know this is going to sound like a line—yeah, again--but it isn't. I've dated girls, like I told you. But I haven't had anything I'd call a serious relationship, you know? And I'm not usually, like..." He reached out and touched the side of my face, just the barest skim of fingers on skin. "Like I am with you. If I'm not touching you, I'm thinking about when I can touch you. It's crazy."

I stabbed a noodle and ran it around the edge of the plate, keeping my eyes down. "I'm not like this, either. And full disclosure, you know that kind of long-term relationship I talked about the other night? It was my first."

"Your first...?" There was question in his tone, although I wasn't sure exactly what he was asking.

"My first everything." I swallowed, still not able to look at him "In high school, I had a group of friends, and we all hung out. If there were big dances, we just went with each other. I liked guys, but they never liked me back. The ones who did like me, I only liked as friends." I lifted one shoulder in a half-shrug. "So I never ended up having a real first date, a first kiss...I know, loser, right?"

"No." Jesse reached across and captured my fork-free hand. "The girls I dated in high school didn't like me as more than friends, and I felt the same way toward them. I had a huge crush on someone who didn't know I existed. She was dating a guy who was in college, but in my fantasy world, she suddenly saw me and realized I was the one she really wanted." He grinned. "I spent way too many Saturday nights trying to get up the nerve to call her."

"It was her loss." I turned my hand over and laced my fingers into his. "What about in college?"

Jesse grimaced and looked away. "I'd like to say I was

totally focused on academics, but I went a little crazy. My dad and Sarah got married right before I graduated from high school, and even though my parents had been divorced forever, I hated that he had a new family. I was living on my own for the first time, and I partied pretty much all the time. I met girls who didn't care that I wasn't on the football team or popular, and I, um, dated a lot of them."

"And by 'um, dated', you mean--"

"I mean one-night...dates. I'm not proud of it."

I squeezed his hand. "You went off the deep end."

"You might say. By winter break of sophomore year, I was failing three classes, my GPA had tanked and my dad came to visit. He wanted to tell me in person that Sarah was pregnant, and that I needed to get my shit together, because I was acting like a spoiled brat."

"Really?" I always saw Danny as a soft touch. He didn't let Desmond get away with everything, but he was definitely the more permissive parent.

"Oh, yeah. It was good timing, because I was sick of it all anyway. So that spring, I had an insane class schedule. I brought up my grades, and I figured out my major. And I stopped, um, dating so much."

I pushed away my almost-empty plate. "Why did you ask me out? Did you think I was going to be one of those girls you 'um, dated'?"

Jesse smiled. "I'm not going to lie, that first day I saw you, 'um, dating' was definitely on my mind. You were on the sofa, looking all sleepy and soft. I was like..." He sucked in a deep breath. "Like, who is this? And then Dad and Sarah said how great you are. Des never stops talking about you. But I didn't want to get back into the party spiral in grad school. I promised my dad I'd be focused on my classes here, and I didn't want him to think I wasn't."

"What changed your mind?"

He tugged my hand until I slipped off the stool and braced my feet on the floor, closer to him but still leaning on my own chair. "It was three things." He held up one finger. "First, you can cook. I've never met a girl who can do that. Or at least a girl who's as gorgeous as you and can cook." He let go of my hand and snaked an arm around my waist. "Two, you love Joss Whedon. That shows excellent taste." He leaned just a smidge closer to touch his lips to mine. "And last, every time I saw you, I wanted to touch you. To kiss you, or hold your hand, or even just brush past you. It was getting overwhelming. I was either going to ask you out or grab you while you were here taking care of Des. The going out seemed like a better idea."

"It does," I agreed. "I'm glad you did."

"I really like you, Julia." Jesse tightened his hands behind my back and lowered his mouth to my ear. "More than I remember liking anyone, ever. But if I get too much, if you feel like I'm too--" He rubbed up my back. "Too intense, you've got to tell me. I don't want to push you into anything."

I smiled up into his eyes. "Like I said before, do you hear me complaining? I promise. If I start to feel that way, I'll tell you."

"Cool." He hugged me tight for a moment and then shifted back. "I know we should take things slow. At least I keep telling myself we should. You just got out of a relationship, and you were hurt, I know." He slid his hands up my side, grinning. "I still really want to 'um, date' you.

So remember that even if I seem to hold back, I don't want to."

I took a deep breath. "I'll try to remember."

"Then I guess it's dishes time." He stood up and snagged both of our plates. "You cooked, I clean."

Chapter Fourteen

I got home late on that Sunday night, but I was still surprised to see that the room was dark and Ava was in bed, the blanket pulled up over her ears.

"Ave, you sleeping?" I said it softly, and she didn't even stir. Frowning, I hung up my coat and went into the bathroom to change for bed. It wasn't like Ava not to wait up for me. As a matter of fact, when Liam and I were dating, I always had to remember to call her on the rare occasions I spent the night with him, so she didn't worry.

I thought about it as I washed my face, brushed my teeth and pulled on pajamas. Ava had been acting weird since last weekend. She had seemed okay when I'd gotten home Friday night, after my date with Jesse; we had stayed up talking, and the only odd thing was that she hadn't said much about her conversation with Liam after I left. I had expected to hear a full play-by-play, but she'd only shrugged and given me a vague answer.

Something was up, and I wondered if Liam was the cause.

Ava didn't move when I clicked off the bathroom light and climbed into bed. It was a long time before I was able to slow down my mind enough to fall asleep.

Desmond was waiting for me at the window Monday afternoon when I arrived at work. He came running out the door the minute I stepped from the car.

"Doolia!"

I stooped to catch him, but he wriggled from my arms and grabbed my hand. "Come and see!"

He dragged me toward the kitchen, where Sarah stood, learning against the counter, smirking.

"Slow down, buddy." I managed to stop long enough to shut the door behind me and drop my bag on a chair. "Where's the fire?"

He giggled and kept tugging at me. "Not a fire, a kitty!" He knelt by a small round cushion, where a tiny gray kitten was sprawled, sound asleep.

"Oh, Des!" I sank down next to him and touched the cat with the tip of my finger. "Who is this?"

"Choo-Choo." Desmond leaned over and buried his face in her fur. "Nanny and Poppa gave her to me."

I glanced up at Sarah, who rolled her eyes. "True story."

"Did you even know they were going to do that?" I

dropped onto my backside and leaned against the wall.

"Oh, yeah, they called last week to ask me. Well, more like beg me. He's wanted a cat so much. They have a neighbor whose cat, um--" She glanced at her son. "Well, she got into trouble. And they needed homes for the kittens, so here we are."

"Choo-Choo?" I stroked the kitten's delicate paw.

"Oh, it could have been worse. He wanted Caboose at first. We decided she's gray, like the smoke that comes out of the old locomotives."

"She's my kitty, and I being vewy dentle with her." Desmond demonstrated his gentleness by petting her between the ears with two chubby fingers. "See? She's a baby. You have to be dentle."

"I will, I promise." I kissed the top of his head and got to my feet. "Did you have a good visit with your parents?"

"Yes, we did. We stayed too late. We didn't get home until almost midnight, so everyone slept in this morning. Danny was late getting to class, and Des and I have been dragging around all morning." She dropped her voice. "He'll be good for an early nap, I think."

"Gotcha." I searched for something else to say. Sarah and I had an easy relationship, but I wasn't sure how she felt about me dating her stepson. Jesse kept saying she and his dad were fine with it, but still...men didn't always pick up the nuances that women did.

"I didn't even get to the grocery store this morning. I took out a chicken to defrost, but I don't have anything done for you to put in the oven."

"Why don't you let me make something?" I suggested. "Maybe chicken and dumplings?"

"Oh, Jules, you're my hero. Thank you. That would be awesome. Do you have everything you need for it?"

"Flour and water. I'll try to have it done by the time Dr. Fleming gets home."

"Doolia, come here." Desmond, tiring of the sleeping kitten, returned to snag my hand again. "Come play."

I shot Sarah a rueful glance, and she grinned. "Seems like you have that effect on more than one Fleming male."

I felt heat spread from my face. "I don't--"

She laughed. "I'm just teasing you, Jules. Go play. I'm heading out, catch you later. Des, give Mommy a kiss before you drag off your woman."

"She not my woman, she my Doolia." Des trotted over to plant a kiss on his mother's cheek before leading me to the toy box.

We played trains until Choo Choo woke up, at which point we had to watch her chase her tail and pursue the toy Des dragged in front of her. He giggled as the ball of fluff somersaulted head over rump and then landed on all fours, looking around wildly as though on the hunt.

"That reminds me." I ruffled Desmond's hair. "I need to put on the chicken for your dinner. Want to help me cook?"

"Yes!" He scrambled up and over the table, where he dragged a chair to the counter and climbed up.

"First you need to find me a pot for the chicken. Get me one this big." I held out hands in a decent approximation of a stock pot.

"Okay dokey." He stepped down with care and opened up the cabinet. I saw his little face wrinkle in concentration as he looked at all the choices offered.

While he worked on that, I retrieved an onion and carrot

from the crisper and washed them, taking the outer peel from the onion. I gave each a rough chop just as Des returned.

"Like this?" He presented me with a wok pan.

"Oh, buddy, that one won't work. I know it's the right size around, but I need a pot. Something deeper. C'mere, I'll show you." I took him over and retrieved the silver stock pot. Desmond nodded, a serious look on his sweet face.

He watched as I dumped the chicken into the pot, added the carrot and onion and then covered the whole thing with water.

"And one tablespoon of apple cider vinegar, to bring out the flavor." I measured it into the mixture.

"Can I smell?"

"Sure." Whenever I cooked with Des, I liked to encourage him to smell, touch and taste. He leaned over the large bottle and took a whiff.

"Eww." His nose wrinkled. "That smell yukky."

"You're not wrong, but mixed in with our other ingredients, you won't even know it's there. Okay, onto the stove goes our bird." I hefted the pot over a burner and turned it on low.

I caught Des yawning as I washed my hands.

"I think it's nap time, baby boy. Want to go read some books?"

"I not a baby." He rubbed at his eyes with one fist, while his lip stuck out.

"Oh, right. Big boy. Still, it's time. Run up and go potty, and I'll meet you on your bed with your books."

We hadn't even gotten through half of the first book before he was snoring. I tucked his favorite airplane blanket around his shoulders and pulled the door shut.

Slipping downstairs, I checked for the kitten before I sank onto the sofa. She was under the coffee table, her little rump wiggling as she prepared to attack my feet. When she leaped, I scooped her up and snuggled the little furball against my chest.

"It's nap time, kitty." I curled my legs beneath me and lay my head on the arm of the couch. "Don't you want to rest?"

Apparently she did, because she began to purr as she nuzzled my hand. My eyes slid shut, and I drifted to sleep.

It was only moments later, I was sure, when I felt the brush of lips over my cheek. I batted it away, and the kitten mewed in protest as I shifted.

"Didn't I tell you what happens when I find you all sleepy and warm?" The words were low and intimate, followed up with soft kisses down my neck. I breathed deep and recognized Jesse's scent.

"Mmmm." I kept my eyes closed. "You smell good. But be careful. The guy I'm seeing lives here, and he might not like it if he catches us together like this."

He paused for just a minute, and I snuck a look at his face through my eyelashes. I wasn't sure if I'd gone too far. I was seeing him, after all; we'd been together the night before and had another date this weekend. Still, neither of us had said anything about being exclusive, unless I counted our first date, when Jesse had asked if I were seeing anyone else.

To my relief, he was grinning, and those dimples were in full view. He plunged his hands to my ribs and tickled.

"Oh, really? The guy you're seeing, huh?"

I sucked in a breath and tried to push his hands away. "No tickling! All right, all right. But stop. You're upsetting

Choo Choo."

As if in response, she stood on my chest, arched her back and stretched, glaring at Jesse.

"Choo Choo? Is that what Desmond named him?"

"Her, actually, and yes. Did you know he was getting a kitten?"

"Yeah, Sarah told me before they left yesterday. She's cute." He picked her up with one hand and rubbed his face against her soft fur, much as Des had done earlier.

When the kitten began to squirm, he set her down on the floor, and she stalked off toward the kitchen. Jesse turned his attention back to me.

"You are way too tempting, lying here like this." He was still wearing his coat, and I could feel the chilled air coming off it.

"You're cold." I found one of his hands and rubbed it between both of mine.

"I am." He leaned over me, bringing his face very close to mine. "I think you should warm me up."

Without warning, he pulled his fingers away and stuck both of his hands under my shirt, against my warm skin.

"Oh, my God." I hissed the words, careful to keep my voice down so we didn't wake Des. "What are you doing? Your hands are like ice!"

"But you're toasty. Sharing body warmth is a good thing." He smiled lazily into my eyes and began moving his hands around, from my sides to my stomach. I sucked in my muscles there, trying to avoid the cold. That only encouraged him to move higher, to the edge of my bra. As his fingers teased there, he brought his mouth down to cover mine.

Jesse kissed with abandon, always. I smiled against his

lips even as he coaxed mine open and sought my tongue with his. I brought up my hands to the back of his neck, and then changed my mind and found the hem of his shirt.

Beneath the gray thermal, he was all muscles and planes, and I traced my fingers upward, with slow precision. I knew he liked my touch, as his lips moved even more aggressively over a low groan.

He shifted to kiss down my neck, pausing as always at the hollow where my clavicle formed a perfect U. As his tongue circled the pulse there, he slipped his fingers beneath the band of my bra, teasing and tempting until my breasts filled his hands.

"Jesse." I could hear the want in my own voice. "Jesse, Des is upstairs asleep. And your dad could come home any minute."

He groaned again and dropped his head onto my chest. His hands were still trapped within my bra, and he moved one thumb just close enough to graze a nipple. I arched back. The last thing I wanted to do was push him away—or stop, for that matter—but I knew we had to be aware of where we were. I didn't want to lose my job or put Jesse in an awkward position with his dad and Sarah.

"I really don't want to move." His voice was muffled against me. "You know how I said I wanted to 'um, date' you the first time I saw you here? I feel the same way right now."

I fingered his curls, smiling at the silkiness. "Yeah, me, too. But we need to be smart, right? If your dad came in right now--"

"I know." Jesse slid his hands out from under my shirt and pushed up. "Okay." He took a deep breath, and I giggled when I saw his nose twitch. I knew what was coming next.

"Mmmm, what smells so good?"

I swung my legs around to sit up next to him. "That's your dinner. I'm making chicken and dumplings for you guys. Matter of fact, I better go get started on the dumplings before it gets any later."

He followed me into the kitchen, hanging his jacket on the coat tree and then leaning against the counter as I lifted the lid from the steaming pot. I breathed in the aroma with my eyes closed.

"Yum. This just needs about another half hour." I turned around. Jesse was looking at me with an odd expression on his face.

"What? Is my hair sticking up?"

"You know when I tell you all the time that you're pretty?"

"Yeah." I tilted my head, waiting to hear what he was getting at. Every time he left, or I left, or we were on the phone or texting, he ended our conversation with those same words.

"I was wrong. You're not just pretty. You're beautiful."

I stood still for a full silent moment, unable to say a word over the tightness in my throat. I didn't have any illusions about my looks—I was ordinary on my good days—but the way Jesse looked at me, I felt gorgeous.

I smiled at him, darting just close enough to drop a quick kiss on his cheek and move out of reach. "Thank you."

"Come back here and thank me better."

Laughing, I pulled down the flour. "Ah, no. While I am most appreciative, I stand by my no-making-out-in-your-parents'-house rule. Sorry."

"Can't blame a guy for trying." He stuck his fingers into the front pockets of his jeans. I measured flour into a large glass bowl, added the water and mixed them up.

"What are you making now?"

"The dumplings." I sprinkled flour onto the wooden cutting board and turned the ball of dough out. "In the drawer behind you, there's a rolling pin. Can you hand it to me?"

"Now that one I know." Jesse rummaged in the drawer and produced the simple pin. "Voila."

"Excellent." I concentrated on moving the pin evenly across the board. "I make rolled dumplings, but some people prefer the dropped. They're a little easier, but I don't think they taste as good." I rinsed off my hands, found a knife and began cutting the sheet of dough into rectangles.

"What time do you get off work?"

I glanced at Jesse over my shoulder. "Um, usually about five, or whenever Danny gets home. Why?"

"Stay for dinner with us."

I turned around, drying my hands on a paper towel. "I don't know, Jesse. Sarah and your dad might not like that. You know...I'm their employee."

Jesse rolled his eyes. "Yeah, you work for them. That doesn't mean you can't eat with us. It's not like a serfdom or whatever. You're not the hired help. And you wouldn't be eating with us as the nanny. You'd be here as my girlfriend."

I stopped moving again, my butt up against the counter opposite Jesse. "I'm your girlfriend?"

"Aren't you? I mean, we're dating, right?"

"We're dating, yes. We're just not 'um, dating'."

"I'll never live that down, will I?"

"Probably not." I slid the chicken pot off the burner and

began straining the stock.

"Well, anyway. I want you to eat with us. You're making dinner, you should be able to eat it, too. If you don't stay, I probably won't be able to see you again until Sunday, at the Super Bowl party."

My stomach dropped a little. I had hoped we might be able to hang out this week, even though I knew we both were busy with classes. With Liam, it had been unusual for us to go more than a day or two without seeing each other, either at a meal or between classes. Which gave me a twinge, remembering his accusation at the birthday party that I should have realized something was up when we went so long without communicating.

Jesse was still speaking, and I brought my mind back to what he was saying.

"My mom called this morning. She's having some sort of plumbing issue at the house, and she doesn't trust the guy who did the work. She wants me to come home and look at it." He held up his hand. "I know, I know. It's just her way to get me up there. But I promised I'd go."

"Hey." I smiled at him. "Don't worry. I understand." I set aside the chicken and moved the pot back to the burner, turning it up. "When are you going?"

"I figured I'd leave Friday right after class, spend Saturday with her, and then drive back Sunday morning, so I'll be home for the game."

"Okay." I began picking the meat from the bones, keeping my eye on the stock.

"So see, you should stay tonight." He came up behind me and slid his hands around my waist. I was helpless to move, my hands covered in chicken grease, and I shivered as he moved his fingers over my ribs.

"Jesse, you're evil."

"Hmmm?" He feigned innocence, even as he dipped his head to the side of my neck.

"Big bro!"

Neither of us had heard Desmond come into the kitchen, but there he stood, his hair sticking up and his blanket clutched in one arm. I bit my lip and squirmed away from Jesse, moving to the sink to rinse my hands.

Jesse stopped me with a hand on my shoulder. "You keep working, I got the rug rat." He turned around and picked him up, spinning the squealing boy in a circle. "So, little dude! I hear you got a new friend. Where's that kitty?"

Desmond glanced around. "I don't know. Doolia, where's Choo Choo?"

"She was here a minute ago. Check in the living room, you two."

"Let's go look for her and let Jules cook, okay." He winked at me over his brother's shoulder, and I watched them disappear around the corner.

Chapter Fifteen

As much as I worried, Danny didn't even blink when Jesse told him I was staying for dinner.

"Jules cooked us dinner, so I asked her to stay." He looked up at his father from the floor, where he and Des were building a block labyrinth for the kitten.

Danny nodded. "Cool. I'm going to get changed and then pour some wine." He sniffed, long and appreciatively. "Julia, that smells divine. Can't wait to eat it." He headed up the steps, and Jesse shot me an I-told-you-so look.

I dropped another flat dumpling into the rolling broth and watched it bob to the surface. Outside, dusk was falling, painting the woods a smudgy gray. I listened to the boys laughing as they tried to convince Choo Choo to walk through the narrow path of blocks. All of that, combined with the aroma of dinner cooking and the warmth of the kitchen, gave me an odd pang of familiarity. I hadn't realized how much I missed home—the feeling of being at home—until that moment.

"Okay, little bro, let's clean up the blocks before Mommy gets here." Jesse stood up and came into the kitchen, leaning over my shoulder to see what I was doing.

"Don't touch," I warned him, glancing back as I dropped in the last dumpling.

"That's not what you were saying earlier." He whispered the words into my ear, but I elbowed him all the same.

"If you don't behave, I'm not staying for dinner."

He stepped back, hands raised. "I'll be the perfect gentleman, I promise."

"Hmph. We'll see."

But he did behave. Sarah came in a few minutes later, just in time to help me finish up dinner. We sat down to eat with the same chaos I'd known growing up: everyone getting drinks, trying to settle Des into his booster seat, moving the plates onto the table and trying to avoid tripping over the kitten, who wanted to be underfoot. Jesse caught my eye and smiled.

It wasn't a bit uncomfortable. Danny talked about his classes, and Sarah told us funny stories about her clients. Jesse sat next to me, but he kept his hands to himself, except for a few reassuring touches to my leg under the table.

When we finished and I rose to clear the table, Sarah fixed me with narrowed eyes.

"Jules, maybe you didn't notice, but you're off the clock. No more work."

"I don't mind helping--" I began, but Jesse took my

hand.

"You heard the woman. Sit down. I'll help with the dishes."

"We're okay, Jesse. Thanks. Why don't you both go do something fun?"

He grinned, tugging at my hand. "That sounds like an order. Come on."

"Where are we going?" I had asked the question twice in the last ten minutes, and each time, Jesse only smiled at me and shook his head.

"It's a surprise," he said now, turning onto the highway. "You're familiar with the concept, right?"

"Yeah, but surprises haven't worked out so well for me lately," I muttered under my breath. "I don't deal well with not being prepared."

"Don't you trust me?"

"Mostly."

He laughed and took the next exit.

"Are you taking me off into the woods to murder me? Because if so, I need to text Ava and let her know. She worries."

"Yeah, that's what I'm doing. You got me."

I saw lights ahead, and Jesse glanced sideways at me.

"One of the guys in my motor disorders class told me about this. I thought it would be something different, and fun, too. I hope." He pulled into the parking lot of a large warehouse building. "How do you feel about ice hockey?"

I raised my eyebrows. "I love it. I don't watch the games on TV so much, but I like the in-person ones. Is that what we're doing? But where?"

Jesse opened his door and came around to do the same to mine. "Right here. This is a farm league, or the closest thing the NHL has to them. The Pennsville Flash."

He took my hand as I slid off the seat into the frigid night. "This is very cool, Jesse. I'm sorry for doubting you."

He rubbed his thumb over the back of my gloved hand. "I had to think of something to get us out of the house. Because what I really wanted to do was go watch TV in the guest house, and pick up where we left off this afternoon. But I figured if I want a relationship with you, it has to be more than just that."

I smiled up at him and leaned in to kiss his cheek. "I appreciate that. Not that I wouldn't have enjoyed your other idea, too. But you're right. I like spending time with you, no matter what we do."

The arena was older, and the crowd was sparse, but the action on the ice was just as intense as a professional game. Jesse laughed at my fervor; I was hoarse from yelling by the end of the first period.

"You're crazy!" he shouted in my ear, over the organ music playing a fight song.

"What's the point of coming if you're not going to support your team?"

He pulled me closer and tipped my chin up. "I like your passion." He dropped his lips onto mine.

"I'm passionate about many things," I murmured against his mouth.

He grinned, and his dimples flashed. I reached up and

touched his cheek.

"Do you know what those dimples do to me? From the first time I met you...I've wanted to kiss you there, to run my tongue over those little indents..."

The blue in Jesse's eyes deepened. "You say things like that, and it makes me regret that we didn't just stay home tonight.

I smiled sweetly. "Something to look forward to, next time."

It was after ten when we pulled into the Flemings' driveway. Jesse pulled his truck up alongside my car.

"Back to your coach, m'lady. Door-to-door service, with a smile."

"Thank you, kind sir. Not only for the service, but for a good time tonight. You rocked it. Next time you surprise me, I'll trust you, I promise."

"Good." He unlatched his seatbelt. "Then that should earn me a hot good-night kiss, right?"

"That isn't earned. That's just a given." I undid my seatbelt, too, and slid to the middle of the seat. Jesse reached down to unbutton my coat.

"What are you doing?"

"My hands are cold again." He slipped them against my side, rubbing up and down. I shivered.

"But now I'm cold," I complained.

"Well, I guess I should do something about that." He moved his hands around to my back and pulled me closer.

"Shared body heat is the most effective, you know. I thought we covered that this afternoon."

"Mmmhmm." I arched my neck to meet his lips. "I'm getting warmer already."

"I feel that. In fact, I think you're putting off enough heat for me to take it up a notch." Before I could protest, his hands were under my shirt against bare skin, and his mouth smothered anything I had to say.

I raked my fingers through his hair and relaxed against his arms, enjoying the lazy interplay of our tongues and feel of his fingers as they teased my spine.

"I should go," I sighed a few minutes later as his tongue trailed down my neck. "Ava will worry. At least I think she will."

Jesse raised his head, frowning in the dim light of the truck cab. "What do you mean?"

"I don't know. She's been...funny the last week or so. Like something's bothering her, but she won't tell me. She says it's nothing. Or she avoids me."

"She's not upset about us, is she? Didn't I make a good impression?"

I shook my head. "No, she liked you. I'm not sure what's going on, but I need to get to the bottom of it."

"You'll figure it out. She seems like a reasonable person."

"She is. She's been my best friend...almost like another sister. I'd never want to hurt her."

"Then I guess you really do have to go. Talk to her. Work it out."

I smiled up at him. "You're pretty amazing. For a guy."

"Gee, thanks." He held the back of my neck and kissed

me once more, hard and searing. "That will have to hold us both until Sunday."

I drew a shaky breath. "Okay then. Text me when you get up to New York?"

"Sure—but I'll talk to you this week. Before I go."

He held my door and stood alongside as I climbed into my own car, and when I looked in the rearview mirror at the end of the driveway, he was still standing just outside the house, in the dim porch light, watching me go.

Chapter Sixteen

I didn't talk to Ava that night, because once again, she was asleep when I got home. She had an early class on Tuesdays, but I intentionally set my alarm so that I was awake before she left.

"Hey, what are you doing up?" She stepped out of the bathroom in jeans and a long sleeved thermal shirt, wet hair combed back from her face.

"I was hoping to catch you before you left. I feel like we keep missing each other the last few days."

"Oh." Ava rolled up her sweats and socks and tossed them into her laundry basket. "I guess so."

"Ave, what's up? I know something is. Can we talk about it? Are you mad at me?"

"No." She sat down on the edge of her bed and pulled on clean socks. "Of course I'm not."

"Then what is it?"

She bit the side of her lip. "It's nothing you did, Jules. It's me. But can we talk about it this afternoon? I promise. I'll meet you at Beans after my last class, okay? Like around four?"

"Okay." I pulled the blankets up around my chin and dozed again until the door closing woke me up.

I only had one class, just after noon, so I had a lazy morning of catching up on homework and updating the blog. I had put up Marcus' story over the weekend, and it was getting huge response.

Writing my own story was on the agenda for today, but I hesitated. The time I spent with Jesse had taken the edge of my rage against Liam, and maybe I didn't need to name names. When I sat back and thought about it rationally, all it would do was hurt Liam and make me look like a loser. There wasn't any winner here.

On impulse, I grabbed my coat, shoved my feet into my shoes and made the short walk over to Dr. Turner's office. I knew she didn't have formal open hours on Tuesday mornings, but I took a chance, and happily, she was there.

"Ms. Cole, this is a surprise." She looked at me over her glasses, but the smile on her face softened the words.

"Do you have a minute, Dr. Turner? I know office hours aren't until tomorrow, but I had a question."

"Of course. Close the door, take a seat."

I shut the glass door, shed my coat and perched on the imitation leather chair across from her desk.

"How's the project going?"

I made a face. "That's why I'm here. It's going well. I mean, we're getting a lot of response, and people are commenting on our posts. There's been discussion about the site on the related social media, and most of it is constructive. Some of it isn't." I frowned, remembering some of the bashing posts I'd read that morning, both from women hating on the guys and men calling our site 'loser chick sob story heaven'.

"That doesn't surprise me at all. What you're revealing can be painful to both sides, to the victim and the perpetrator, as it were. Plus, you have to take into account point of view. What a sensitive young girl might take as a cruelty might not seem such a big deal to the boy who thinks he's doing the right thing."

I nodded. "I'm starting to see that. Lots of the comments are saying we're only telling one side of the story. And because it's anonymous, that's all we can do." I took a deep breath. "And that's what I wanted to talk to you about. I need to make a decision about publishing a story, and I want to make the right choice."

"All right." Dr. Turner smiled and tilted her head. "Shoot."

"This is a story that's going to be recognizable to most students on campus. But the submitter wanted us to use names, too. Make it clear exactly who the guy was. Is, I mean. Lose the anonymity."

"Aha." She pursed her lips. "Go on. Why does this person want to be open about the names? Keeping it private was one of the conditions of your site, I thought."

"Well, it is. But she wanted—or needed, maybe—closure, and she thought this might be the way to get it. The guy who did it, who hurt her, he hasn't ever apologized or even admitted he was wrong. I guess maybe she thought this was a way to show him how she felt. Make him feel her pain."

"Mmmmhmmm." Dr. Turner tapped her fingers on the desk. "So we're talking revenge here."

I flushed and kept my eyes to the carpet. "I suppose so."

"Ah." She sighed, running her hands over the neat bun of black hair at the back of her head. "Well, I don't think that's unexpected, given the name of the blog. It was only a matter of time. It's a fine line between providing a forum for people to share and giving them an outlet for...well, retribution."

"So do you think I shouldn't do it?"

"Ms. Cole, I'm not here to be your journalistic conscience. I'm teaching you, or at least I hope I am, to develop your own." She looked into the distance, over my shoulder. "It's hard when it's personal, isn't it?"

My heart beat a little faster. "Um, I'm sorry?"

She smiled, her eyes full of understanding. "Students tend to think the gossip stays within their own body. But we professors hear a good deal more than you give us credit for. Maybe I'm making a leap, but I know what happened in December. Unless I am far less perceptive than I credit myself, I don't think you're discussing someone else's story here. I think you're talking about your own."

I swallowed hard. "I'm sorry, Dr. Turner. I wasn't trying to lie to you, I just wanted to have a little distance--"

"Then take a look at that distance. If this were in fact another submitter, writing to you with the request that you publish her story complete with names, what would you tell her?"

I took a deep breath. "I guess I would tell her it's not our policy, and ask her why she felt it was important."

"Which is what I asked you. And you mentioned the need for closure." She rolled her eyes, and my mouth dropped.

"I happen to detest all that psychological babble at times, Ms. Cole. Not that I don't think some of it has merit, but in this case, as in many others, we use the idea of closing a chapter of our lives to justify questionable action."

"So you don't think people should be held accountable for their actions? Even when they hurt others?"

"Of course I do. That's why I went into journalism, after all. Remember I came of age in the Watergate era. Holding people responsible was our rally cry. But in this case, what's the best possible result to telling your story with names, for publishing it with Mr. Bailey's name included?"

"That's what I was thinking this morning. Liam would be embarrassed, sure, but I don't think he'd learn anything. And I might hurt friends of ours, put them in the middle."

"Let's not ignore the elephant in the room, either. Publishing your own story that way does call your journalistic integrity into question, and it would also jeopardize the reputation of your blog. If getting your own revenge was the only reason you decided to tackle this issue, Ms. Cole—and I don't think was—you've let down your readers."

I stretched my neck against the back of the chair and sighed. "No. I mean, it gave Kristen and me the initial idea, but it's not the only reason. And I didn't even intend to use Liam's name in my post until last weekend. He made me really mad. Again."

Dr. Turner shook her head. "Julia, Julia...writing from a

place of strong emotion is not the role of the journalist. We write to evoke response, but not out of our own passion. You know better than that."

"You're right." I clinched my eyes shut. "I'm sorry. I just needed to hear it, I guess."

"Don't apologize. You did what any good journalist would do when she realized she needed distance: you took it outside you, and you asked for input." She paused for a beat. "You remind me of myself, but I'm happy to say you are far more mature than I was, even when I was a bit older than you."

The chair creaked as she leaned back. "I was fresh out of college and working in DC. I met a man through my roommate—she had known him in New York when they both worked there—and I fell madly in love.

"I know, you look at me now and think that's impossible, I'm a dinosaur, but in those days, I was exotic and adventurous and very driven. Men fell at my feet, but I wanted this one. And for a brief time, he wanted me, too."

"I can see that." I smiled. "I can imagine you setting the world on fire."

"Ah." She quirked an eyebrow. "It was a long time ago. But I made a fool of myself over this man, because I thought he loved me as I did him. In the end, I was wrong. I had a choice, after he humiliated me, broke my heart: I knew things, you see, things he wouldn't have wanted to get out. I had a golden opportunity to break a huge story, and by way of that, I would have had my revenge."

I listened, mouth opened in anticipation. "What did you do?"

Dr. Turner closed her eyes. "I wrote the story. I did it in

haze of righteous anger, and I took it to my editor, and he read it. And then he said to me essentially what I am telling you. He killed the story. Oh, it came out later, as it should have, in the right way, broken by someone else who didn't have an axe to grind."

"Did you regret it? Do you think he ever knew that you could have done it and didn't?"

She laughed. "I regretted it every minute for years. I second-guessed it, and I raged at my editor. But ultimately, he was right. My ex went on to break a lot of other hearts, and publishing the story wouldn't have changed that. Something happened to him many, many years later, and I think, as they say, karma is a bitch."

"Did he ever tell you he was sorry?"

"Never. He probably didn't even remember the whole episode. I was just one in a very long list of conquests."

I reached out and touched the top of her hand where it lay on her desk. "I'm sorry, Dr. Turner."

She took a breath and sat a little straighter, smiled just a bit. "Thank you. Life goes on. But if it's any consolation to you that I've been in your position, then I'm glad my story helps." She began fussing with the blotter on her desk, and I took that as my cue to wrap up our meeting.

"Thanks for listening, and for the good advice. I hope someday I can pass it on." I stood and shrugged into my coat.

"Oh, you will. Keep up the good work, Ms. Cole. I've been following your blog. You and Kristen have done a nice job putting it together. I'm glad you're not going to let down your readers or your partner." She gazed at me meaningfully over the top of her glasses, which I understood was a not-subtle reminder that my grade and reputation were not the only ones at stake here.

"Understood. Thanks again."

"Any time." She smiled as I closed the door behind me.

Out in the sunshine, I felt another layer of stress fall away, and I drew in a deep, cleansing breath. It was one of those rare moments when my world felt peaceful and possible.

It lasted until I was right outside the dorm and spied Liam, who was standing in the courtyard, looking up at the windows as though he could see into them.

I wondered if I could walk past without him noticing me. But in my new spirit of peace and love, I decided to try something else.

"Hey. What are you doing here?" Okay, so it maybe sounded a little hostile, but the way I said was more curiosity and less accusation.

He jumped as though I'd hit him. "Julia? My God, don't sneak up on me."

I shook my head. "I didn't sneak up. I was headed into my room. I live here, remember? And I thought it would be nice to say hello. You look like Spiderman about to scale the wall. Are you waiting for someone?"

He squirmed. I never thought I'd see the day, but cool and collected Liam Bailey was decidedly uncomfortable. I remembered Rachel, the freshman girl he'd brought to his birthday party, who now lived in this dormitory, and my stomach turned just a little.

"No. Not really. Just was hoping to run into someone. Maybe."

I smiled, saccharine sweet. "Not me, I take it?"

"No, not you." He said it so definitely that I had to laugh.

"Thanks. I guess you gave up on stalking me? Taking your offer off the table, huh?"

"My offer?" He frowned.

"You know. Booty call without strings. Keeping me off the street. No leftovers to the rabble, right?"

His face turned red, and my mouth dropped open. *Was I really embarrassing him?*

"Julia, I'm sorry. I was wrong to say that the other day. You just—I was dealing with crap, and yeah, seeing you with other guys worried me. It freaked me out a little. Giff jumped all over me, and I know I need to just leave you alone. Okay?"

My world, so peaceful moments ago, suddenly felt off-kilter.

"I think I must have stepped into an alternate reality. One where Liam Bailey actually knows how to apologize. And shows remorse."

He made a face at me. "What are you talking about? I apologize. The whole time we were going out, I did nothing but apologize to you. I could never do the right thing."

"No, you always just asked if I were still pissed at you and then played the—no. You know what, Liam? I'm not doing this. You just did a decent thing, and I'm not going to ruin it by second-guessing everything. Thank you. And now, before any other bizarre world shit goes down, I'm going upstairs to lie down until class."

I turned to push open the door, and Liam called to me.

"Are you--" He cast his eyes up again at the windows. "Is Ava waiting for you up there? Are you going to lunch with her?"

I shook my head. "No, she's in class all day. I have the

room to myself. Why?" Suspicion crept into my voice as I wondered what game Liam was playing now.

"Nothing. I, just, uh, was going to ask her about a class. A question I had. I'll catch her later. No problem. See you, Julia."

He turned and sprinted down the walkway before I could say anything. I shrugged and went inside, shaking my head.

This had been the oddest day.

Chapter Seventeen

Ava was already sitting down when I got to Beans a little after four. She waved to me, and I cut around several people in line to get to the table.

"I ordered you a mocha latte on ice. Even though I think you're nuts to drink cold drinks in the winter."

"I'm quirky, what can I say?" I sank into the chair across from her. "Thanks. And it's not that cold outside today. The sun was really warm."

"Yeah." Ava picked up the paper wrapper from her straw and began folding it into tiny squares. Her eyes focused on the task, but I didn't think she was really seeing it.

"Ave." I reached across to squeeze her hand. "What's going on? Come on, this is me, Jules, who knows everything about you and loves anyway. And who's been driving you nuts being needy and insane for the last three months."

"Only the last *three* months?" She lifted an eyebrow at me, and I grinned.

"Thanks, I love you, too. But seriously, tell me what's going on."

Ava licked her lips and sucked in a breath through her nose. "Jules, I do love you, and you know that, right? You're my best friend, ever, and we might joke about that or whatever, but you know it's true. I would never, ever hurt you for anything in the world."

My heart was beginning to pound a little bit. I sat back in my chair. "Okay, yes. I know all that. Ave, you're freaking me out."

She pushed away her drink toward the middle of the table. "That Friday night, when you first went out with Jesse, Liam came over just as you were leaving."

"Right." I frowned. "You said he talked to you about me being out with all those other guys, and you told him to mind his own business."

"Yes. That's what happened. To a certain point. You left, and he was standing in the hallway. I didn't want to let him into our room. He said he needed to talk to you about how you were acting, that people were talking about you, blah, blah, blah. And I kept saying it was none of his business, and he should leave.

"And then that girl Rachel, the freshman? She was walking down the hall. And she saw him there, and he saw her, and so he asked me if he could come in. She looked upset, and I didn't want to deal with their drama, so I let him in."

She dropped her head into her hands. "I swear, Jules, I

never thought—I figured he would come in, finish what he was blabbing on about, and then leave. I just wanted a quiet night to do my homework."

"Okay." I was still lost, still confused.

"So he sat down on my bed, and I sat on my chair, and he told me Rachel was giving him a hard time, calling him, texting, and he couldn't shake her loose. I laughed and said he seemed to have a hard time knowing how to end relationships, and he said she wasn't a relationship, she was just big mistake."

"Hmph. A big mistake he was making out with in front of all our friends just to shake *me* loose. What goes around..."

"Yeah, I pretty much said the same thing. And he said he knew it, but it was complicated, and he just wanted to talk to you, to make sure you weren't going to do something dumb because of him."

"Same old song," I snorted. "Ava, I still don't see--"

"I'm not done yet." She said it so grimly that I snapped my mouth closed.

"After that, I don't know, we were just talking. I had forgotten how we used to talk when you guys were dating. I didn't realize I'd kind of missed that. And then I got out some wine, and we were just...talking.

"And then he said something funny, I don't even remember what it was, and I laughed. When I looked at him, he...umm, he had a strange expression, and then...he leaned over and kissed me."

"Oh, my God! Are you freaking kidding me? And here I was thinking he might be changing...Ave, I am so sorry. He's an asshole."

"Jules, you don't understand." Misery etched her face.

"It wasn't just him kissing me. I kissed him back. And more."

I'm not sure what my face looked like at that moment, but it was probably a study in shock.

"More? What do you...? Did you sleep with him, Ave?"

"No." Her eyes were bleak. "But we—there was kissing. Lots of it. And...touching. When I finally made him stop—made us stop—he said he should go, and he would call me the next day. But I told him he shouldn't, that you—I couldn't do that to you."

I laid my hands flat on the table and stared at them, breathed in and out once. I looked up at Ava. Of everything Liam had done to me, of every way he had hurt me, this was the worst. Not only because of the pain and betrayal I felt, but because of the guilt I saw in my best friend's eyes.

"Ave, I'm not mad. Not at you, anyway. I'm—I'm surprised. Shocked. Um, I don't know what to say."

She leaned forward, almost pleading. "I didn't, either. This is Liam. After he left and I could think straight, I realized how stupid I was. That he was playing me, probably just to hurt you. Then he called me when he got back to his room, and he asked me to meet him the next morning for breakfast, somewhere off campus. I said I could never do anything to hurt you, and he told me you were with so many other guys, you wouldn't even notice."

I heaved a sigh and shook my head. "Ava, this is a mess. I get—at least, I mostly get—how you could kiss him. He's hot, he's good, and you're not the first girl he's conned into a make-out session or worse. But why on earth didn't you tell him to go to hell when he called?"

She lifted one shoulder. "Jules, he was so sweet. When

he said—what he said, I wanted to believe him. I hadn't made up my mind when you came back from the wrestling thing. But when you told me what he'd offered, I knew he'd been lying to me. All week, though, ever since, he's been calling me, trying to see me. Waiting for me after class. I saw him once or twice. I feel so stupid, Jules, and I still do. I'm so, so sorry. Can you forgive me?"

I sipped my now-watery drink. "Ava, there's nothing to forgive. I don't care what Liam does now. I only care about you. If I really thought you and Liam could—well, could work—I'd deal with it. But he's only out to hurt you."

"But everyone knows you don't go out with your friends' ex. Ever. What's the matter with me? I'm a horrible bitch."

"You are so not. Liam is a master manipulator, Ave. That's a given. I just wish you had told me right away and not agonized."

She rubbed her forehead. "It was just temporary insanity, I guess."

We finished our drinks in silence, and even on the way back to the dorm, neither of us spoke.

Since I never had dated before Liam, the idea of a boy coming between one of my friends and me was strange. I wanted to be angry with Liam again, to go back to the place where revenge felt like a perfect option.

At the same time, something was still bothering Ava. I knew she felt regret, remorse—now the surprise trip to church for confession last weekend made sense—but she also seemed sad. When we got back to our room, she changed into sweats, stuck in her ear buds and climbed into bed with one of her huge textbooks.

I worked on homework until the darkening room and my growling stomach made me think of dinner. I glanced across the room at Ava. She was propped against pillows, with a book on her knees, but she wasn't reading. Instead she was staring into the distance, a frown wrinkling her forehead.

I tossed a pillow at her, to get her attention. She jumped and then took out the ear buds.

"What was that for?"

"It's time for dinner. You want me to get takeout and bring it back? You're looking pretty comfy over there."

She shrugged. "I'm not very hungry. Whatever you want to do."

I climbed off my bed and onto Ava's. "What's wrong? You're not still worried I'm upset, are you? I'm not. Not at you."

She didn't meet my eyes. "No. I'm just...disappointed in myself. All this time I've been so focused on the important things. I haven't given boys a thought. Well." She gave me a half-smile. "Maybe a thought or two. But I've stayed on my path. And then this guy who I know for sure is a jerk and a player comes along and kisses me, and suddenly I'm no better than any other lovesick girl."

"Lovesick?" I wrinkled my forehead.

"It's a figure of speech."

I laid my head on her shoulder. "Ave, you are the most amazing person I know. I see the looks you get when we're out. You're gorgeous, smart and funny. All you'd have to do is let it happen, and guys would be falling at your feet. But you have a plan, and you stay focused. Just because you have one little slip doesn't mean you've failed." I sighed. "I can tell you Liam Bailey isn't just a guy. He might be a class A ass, but the boy knows how to kiss. And what to say to a girl, when he's in the mood to be charming. So don't beat yourself up."

If anything, Ava looked more miserable.

"I didn't tell you. I had a meeting today with Dr. Turner. I've decided not to write that story for the blog. At least, I'm not naming names."

"What made you change your mind?"

I shook my head. "I don't know. I guess it was realizing that I've moved on. I had such a good time with Jesse last night. It's easy, and it feels right, you know? Not the constant up and down and angst there was with Liam. I ran it all by Dr. Turner, and she gave me some good advice."

"So all the revenge plans are abandoned?" Ava worried the side of her lip between her teeth.

"I guess. When I saw him this afternoon, I--"

Ava shifted on her pillows, turning so she could see me. In the process, I nearly fell off the bed.

"You saw Liam this afternoon?"

"Yeah. Sorry, I guess I forgot, with us talking about everything else. He was standing outside the building here when I got back from seeing Dr. Turner."

"What was he doing here?"

I shook my head. "I have no idea. He was kind of cagey about it. No, that's not true. He was, like, nervous. And he apologized for the other day. I mean, really said he was sorry, not the typical cover-his-ass-and-not-take-any-blame crap. I almost fell over."

"He apologized?" Ava sat up.

"Yeah, for what that's worth."

She narrowed her eyes at me, and I could tell something was going on in her brain. When she spoke, it was with a new calm.

"Jules, maybe your revenge plans aren't quite over yet."

"Ava, that's crazy."

"No, it's not. It's perfect. Everything else we were thinking about before was so haphazard—you showing up all over campus with different guys hoping to make him jealous, even writing about him on the blog—all of that felt sloppy. But this, this is exactly right."

"It's not fair to you. Ave, you don't need to do this."

"Oh, I think I do. And it's fair to me. He decided to include me in his games. He wants to mess with me? Good. Now it's time for him to get a big old tablespoon of his own medicine. And isn't it perfect that my birthday just happens to be in two weeks?"

"The last thing I want to do is plan another birthday party. You know what people are going to be saying. It'll bring up everything from December again."

"Exactly. So it'll be fresh in people's minds. And when Liam walks in, every eye will be on him."

"Ava, are you sure...?"

"Stop it, Jules. I'm positive. Put it into action. Get the girls on the floor to help you with the plans and the decorations. You can handle the food. We can do it in the main lounge here." She smiled, and the look in her eye made me shiver. "And don't worry about Liam. I'll deliver a special invitation to him."

"God, Ave, you scare me. Remember you're supposed to use your powers for good, not evil."

She laughed. "This is for the good. Liam Bailey is going to learn what happens when you screw with the wrong women."

Chapter Eighteen

The buzzing of my phone on Sunday morning interrupted a sweet dream I was having about a sunny beach and one of those fruity drinks with a little paper umbrella.

Muttering under my breath, I reached for the phone with my eyes still closed and swiped it on before realizing it was a text, not a call. I squinted at the screen, trying to focus my eyes on the tiny words.

Almost home. Stopped for gas. When can you come over?

I grinned. Jesse. And he must have missed me.

You're early!

Left first thing.

I wondered how that had gone over with his mom. The little clock in the corner of my phone showed it was just past nine, which meant he must have left New York around six or so.

I have to stop at grocery 1st.

I'll come get you, we'll go together. Be there in 30 mins?

I scrambled to sit up. Thirty minutes? Only a guy would expect anyone to be ready in half an hour. I tried to think clearly for a moment and then made a decision.

I'll be downstairs waiting.

I could see my breath as I stood outside the dormitory, but the sun was almost warm. I stood basking in it, bundled up against the chill air but still thinking fondly of my dreams about the beach.

It was so quiet on campus that I heard Jesse's truck before I saw him. He pulled up to the curb, and I sprinted over.

He came around to open my door, meeting me with a hug first.

"Are you frozen, standing out here?"

"Just about. Are you going to let me in and warm me up?"

A smile curved his lips. "All I've been thinking about since I saw you last was warming you up again. Come on, get in."

I buckled my seat belt as Jesse climbed into his seat. He turned me toward him with a hand on my shoulder.

"Hi. I missed you."

I moved just enough to close the distance between our lips and murmured against his mouth. "I missed you, too. I'm glad you're back."

His kiss was slow and languorous, surprising me since Jesse usually kissed as though our lives depended on it. A flash of desire spread over me, and I leaned closer, moving a hand to the back of his neck.

The windows of the truck cab were fogged by the time Jesse broke away, resting his forehead against mine.

"I guess we should get moving." He brushed his knuckles along my face. "Want to tell me how to get to the grocery store?"

"Sure." I leaned back into my seat, catching my breath. "If you go out the main exit, make a right. There's a Shop Rite a few miles down on the left."

Jesse pulled out, maneuvering along the nearly-empty campus roads.

I adjusted the heater vents to blow onto my hands. "How was the visit with your mom?"

He made a face. "I lived. When I first got there Friday night, she was really defensive...like she was ready to pick a fight. If I said anything about Dad or Sarah, she jumped on it. But she calmed down by the next morning, and I actually had a decent time with her. Until I told her I was coming back down here first thing today. Then she started up again." His lips twitched, and I wondered what he wasn't saying.

"Did you tell her...that you were...about me?"

"Yeah. I did." He glanced over at me. "Julia, she's really a terrific person. But she's insecure. So when she hears I'm dating someone down here, someone who works for my dad, she jumps to the conclusion that it's his idea, that he and Sarah set us up so that I'd want to stay down here longer. She just isn't reasonable. But it's not you—it's the situation."

"I understand." I bit my lip.

We turned into the grocery store parking lot. Jesse found a spot in the back and came around to open my door.

"Hey." He slid his arms around my waist before I could climb down from the seat. "Don't worry about the stuff with my mom, okay? Seriously. I'm my own person, always have been. She's just a little nuts." He leaned in to kiss me lightly.

I smiled. "Sorry, I have parent issues. My ex-boyfriend's father was very controlling."

"That's not us." He took my hand and helped me down. "Now let's go fight the mobs and get us some food. I'm starving."

In the end, we went with traditional football fare: wings, potato skins and a variety of dips. Jesse carried the bags into the guest house while I unloaded everything onto the counter.

"I still can't believe you wanted me to buy pre-made wing sauce. Please. I make my own."

"Okay, Julia Child. Just trying to help." He smirked at his own joke. "That's the end of it. Now what?"

"Now we need to cook the wings and the potatoes." I glanced at the clock on the microwave. "But not yet, probably. It's still early. When is everyone coming over?"

"I told them four." Jesse leaned against the wall. "And it's not even twelve yet. Hmm. What are we going to do to kill time between now and then?"

"I can't imagine." I put the sour cream and a block of

bleu cheese into the fridge. "I guess we could play cards."

"We could." He came around into the kitchen and pinned me against the counter. "But I may have a better idea." His hands tightened on my hips, and he nipped at my neck. "Have I mentioned yet how much I missed you this week?"

His mouth was on me before I could answer, kissing me until I couldn't breathe and then moving back down my neck, even as his hands slid under my shirt to pull me flush against him.

I swallowed a moan, feeling the evidence of his desire even through his jeans. We'd been teasing and tantalizing each other for weeks now, and my heart pounded at the thought that today the wait might be over.

Jesse reached around my back and scooped me into his arms. I muffled my squeal of surprise into his shoulder as he carried me to the sofa.

"God, Julia, you make me...I just want to have my hands on you. My mouth." He held me in one arm and used the other hand to palm my breast, lifting my shirt so that it bunched around my neck.

I sucked in a breath as his fingers slipped into the cup of my bra, finding my nipple. His finger grazed there, and his lips feathered over mine, soft as a sigh. Every nerve in my body was electrified.

He shifted so that I lay half on the sofa, half across his legs, never breaking the kiss. His mouth traced a path down my throat, licking and caressing as he went, until he reached his fingers on my breast. He pushed back the cup of my bra, and his lips fastened on the nipple his finger had been teasing.

"Jesse..." I half-moaned his name.

"Jules, you're so beautiful." The vibration of his voice against my breast shot desire and need straight to my core, and I squirmed.

"Julia..." He laid his head on my chest for a beat before moving just enough to see my face. "I know your ex—you said he was your first. I got the feeling maybe he pressured you into that. I don't want to be like him. I want to be with you, in every possible way. But right now, today, I only want to make you feel how gorgeous you are, how desirable..."

His arms still cradling me, Jesse captured the peak of my breast again, his tongue swirling. He raised his mouth away just long enough to grip my shirt and pull it over my head, lifting me a bit, so that he could reach my other breast with his mouth.

I held onto his back, my fingers kneading the hard muscles there. He tongued a path down my stomach before pausing to glance up at me.

"Julia, can we--"

"The bedroom?" I answered what I hoped was his thought. "Please. Yes."

Before the words were quite out of my mouth, he had me in his arms again, kicking open the door and falling with me into his bed.

Every part was alive, on fire. My fingertips itched to touch him, and my skin hummed with need for his fingers, his lips. He paused only long enough to strip off his own shirt with one hand, and then he was next to me again.

He kissed the edge of my breast, just above my bra.

"Your heart is pounding," he murmured.

I flattened my hand on his chest and smiled. "Yours,

too."

He gathered me closer, rolling me to the side and reaching for the hook of my bra. "This is okay?"

I kissed the side of his neck. "It is really, really okay."

Jesse released the hooks and eased the bra away, tossing it to the side of the bed. He drew in a deep breath and then let it out, slowly, so that I could feel warmth tickling my skin.

"You're gorgeous. So..." As if he couldn't wait a moment longer, he brought his mouth and hands back to my breasts, licking circles around my nipples, teasing with his teeth until I was almost shaking with need, writhing in a haze of desire.

He raised his head to look at me as his fingers trailed lower, to the button of my jeans. "Is this good?"

In answer I raised my hips and nodded. Jesse's smile brought out his dimples, and I lifted my hand to trace them.

He unfastened my jeans, lowered the zipper and eased his fingers within, just over the cotton of my underwear. The moment he touched the slickness of my center, I gasped and arched my back, moaning.

"Shhh..." He covered my mouth in a kiss again, his tongue imitating what his hands were doing between my legs. "Shh. Just...feel. I want to make you feel good. Close your eyes, and trust me."

I exhaled and fell back to the pillows, lost in sensation as Jesse tugged my jeans off. He kissed his way down my legs and then back up to my stomach before he slid his fingers beneath my panties moving in sensual exploration.

"God, Jesse, please." I was half-panting as he ignited the bundle of nerves at my center and suckled hard at my breast. "Please..."

"Let it happen. Relax. Feel."

Whispering the words, he moved his fingers lower, plunging them into me. I arched my back, holding my breath and gripping his arm. He dropped his head against my neck, murmuring things I couldn't quite understand against my skin. He made me feel more alive, more beautiful, than I'd ever felt.

Jesse moved his thumb to press into me, and that took me over the edge. I cried out his name, moving in mindless ecstasy against his hand, feeling wave after wave of pure pleasure wash over me as I shook.

And then he was kissing me again, holding my head in place and whispering against my lips.

"Julia...my God."

"I think that's my line," I said, laughing shakily. I reached my hand to touch along the top of his stomach. "Do you want...can I...?"

"Not now." He lay down alongside me, skimming his hand over my skin. "Yes, I want. Very much. But more than that, I needed this to be for you."

I held his face within my hands, kissing him deeply. "Thank you. It was...beyond wonderful. I never..." I licked my lips. "Never had anyone focused on me."

"It's not that I don't want everything. To be with you. But we haven't talked about it. And I know this is still kind of new." Jesse traced one fingertip between my breasts, down my stomach. "I don't want you to feel like I'm pushing you into anything."

I turned onto my side, cuddling into him. "Thank you for that."

"I don't want to bring this up now, but maybe it's the

right time. I told you about my first few years at college, Jules. I did things without thinking them through. Slept with more girls—well, we already talked about that. Since that year, since I turned things around, I haven't been with anyone. I want it to mean something."

I traced the lines of his lip, to where the dimple would be if I could see it now. "I never was with anyone, until Liam. And even then, I wasn't sure. And he didn't force me, I don't want you to think that. But he made me feel like there was something wrong with me if I didn't. He didn't say so, it was just an attitude. So then...I did. I thought, better to just get it over with, and maybe part of me was afraid he would stop wanting me if I didn't. Of course, that didn't really turn out too well, either."

Jesse kissed the top of my head. "Turned out okay for me."

"You're right. Actually, it did turn out, better than I could have thought." I ran my hand over his chest. "Thank you for making me feel beautiful. And for not minding if we wait just a little bit."

"Hey, any time. I'll tell you a secret. There isn't anything sexier than watching your woman enjoy herself, knowing you're the one who's making it happen."

I smiled. "Really?"

"Yup. The only thing that's hotter is seeing her in the kitchen, cooking for you, after you've given her the best orgasm of her life."

"Jesse!" I knew my face was red. It was one thing to do it, quite another to talk about it. "You sexist pig."

"That's me." He swung his legs off the bed, gathered my clothes and tossed them to me. "Get dressed, wench. There's food to prepare before my fellow cavemen get here."

Chapter Nineteen

I had been a little nervous about meeting Jesse's friends from grad school, but they turned out to be a friendly, low-key bunch. Two of the guys brought along their girlfriends. One, Alana, was already working as a teacher at a local elementary school, and the other, Stephanie, who I vaguely recognized, introduced herself as a senior at Birch.

All the food was ready when they showed up, and we munched as we watched the pre-game show. The wings were a big hit.

"Can you please give me this recipe?" Alana wandered into the tiny kitchen as I rinsed off a pan. "I'm trying to learn how to cook, so Jake and I don't have to go out to eat so much. We're saving up to get married."

"That's so great." I turned off the water and dried my hands. "Sure, I'll send you the recipe. It's really easy." I dug out my phone from my purse. "What's your email?"

She rattled it off to me, and I keyed it into my contacts. I was just putting away my phone when there was a knock at the door.

"That must be Cal. He said he had to work late." Jesse opened the door, and a tall boy with longish black hair came in.

"Sorry. Working at a liquor store on Super Bowl Sunday is a bitch." He peeled off his jacket and hung it over a chair. "Did I miss kick-off?"

"No, just about to happen. Cal, you know everyone else here—this is Julia, my girlfriend."

I was still standing behind the counter with Alana, doing a fast clean up before the start of the game, and I smiled at the newcomer. He gave me a nod and a wave, and then a very peculiar look crossed his face.

I realized, when I saw that expression, that I knew Cal. Or at least I had seen him before. He was an Alpha Delt, and I'd met him with Liam. Still, it wasn't a secret that Liam and I had dated, so I wasn't sure why he looked at me so oddly. Unless...if the talk around campus was as bad as Liam had said, maybe he heard something. My stomach turned over. I hadn't done anything wrong, not really. I hadn't seen any other guys since Jesse and I had begun seeing each other, other than the wrestling match, and even that had been perfectly innocent. He'd understand. I hoped.

I finished throwing away the paper plates, wiped down the counters and went into the living room. Jesse was sprawled in one of the easy chairs, and he pulled me down into his lap.

"Nice job on the food, woman," he whispered into my

ear, teasing.

I wriggled against him, trying to elbow his ribs, but he caught my hands in his and brought them to his lips to kiss.

"Thank you. Everything was delicious."

I settled back, laying my head on his chest. "You're welcome. It was the least I could do, after...well, you know."

Jesse didn't say anything, but his face grew slightly red. Taking advantage of the situation, I shimmied a little lower, moving my rear against the growing hardness I felt within his jeans.

He tightened his arms around my middle.

"Behave," he murmured. "I'm not going to be able to stand up now."

"Hmmm." I smiled, barely able to keep from giggling. "Pay attention to the game. You'll feel better soon."

"Is that a promise?"

"Sure."

The game was a good one, with a close score and lots of action. At half time, I served the chocolate chip cookies I'd made that afternoon.

"Man, Jesse, your girlfriend can cook!" I heard one of the guys say.

"Yeah. One of her many skills." There was pride in Jesse's voice. "She's also a really good writer. And she's smart, and she likes to watch sports."

I stood still for a moment. I couldn't remember even one instance when Liam had praised me, either to my face or to someone else. Hearing Jesse do it now almost made me cry.

Since everyone had classes or work the next day, the party broke up as soon as the game ended. I stood with Jesse as he walked his friends to the door. When they were gone, I stood on tip-toe to kiss his cheek.

"Nice party. I'm going to head out, too. It's late."

"And just how are you planning to get back to campus?"

I rolled my eyes. "Crap, I forgot I don't have my car. Well, I guess my wonderful, fabulous, sexy boyfriend is going to drive me."

"He could, or he could just keep you here overnight and then take you back to campus in the morning." Jesse held my hips, bringing me closer.

"Nice try, ace. I've got an early class, and I'm exhausted. My boyfriend kept me working hard all day."

He smiled, dropping light kisses along the side of my face. "That's true. I kept you busy. I'll get our stuff."

He disappeared into his bedroom and returned with both of our jackets. "That doesn't mean I won't push the issue again, though." He helped me with my coat, gently pulling my hair out of the collar. "Even if we don't do anything but sleep, the idea of waking up next to you is pretty exciting."

I shook my head. "You've never seen me in the morning. I'm a hot mess. Ratty hair, bleary eyes and--" I dropped my voice. "Morning breath."

He feigned horror and held up his hands. "I take it back. No overnights for you."

"Jerk." I took his hand, and we went out to the truck.

"Seriously, thank you for making all the food tonight. I'm now the envy of all the SLP grad students." He kept one hand on the steering wheel while the other held mine as he drove.

"At least the ones here tonight. You're welcome. I like cooking for a party, and I don't get to do it very often." Which reminded me of the next party I was throwing.

"By the way, Ava's birthday is coming up. I'm going to give her a party in our lounge at the dorm. Want to come?"

"Sure. Need me to help with anything?"

"I'll let you know when it gets closer, thanks. It'll be a week from Friday, probably at seven."

Jesse lifted our joined hands to kiss my wrist. "I'm hoping I'll talk to you before then. Maybe even see you."

"Well, I'll have to check my schedule. You know I'm very busy." I giggled.

Jesse made a face at me as we drove onto campus. "You're making me regret not tying you to the bed tonight."

"Ha. Just try it, buddy."

We pulled up in front of the dorm, and Jesse let the truck idle. "Home again, home again. Want me to walk you in?"

I shook my head. "No, thanks. It's late, and you need to get home. Plus Ava might be asleep already."

"Hey, that reminds me. Did you ever find out what was bugging her?"

I bit my lip. "Sort of. Some guy was bugging her. I think it's taken care of now."

"Anything I can do? Talk to the jerk?"

"That's sweet, but no, we're handling it for now." I leaned over to kiss his cheek. "I'm going to go in. Talk to you this week?"

"At least. I'll probably see you tomorrow while you're on Des duty." He pulled me into one more searing kiss. "'Night, Jules."

I did see Jesse the next day, but only briefly. He got home later, and I was just about to leave when he pulled into the driveway. I stood next to my car as he jumped out of the truck.

"Damn, I was afraid I was going to miss you."

I hunched my shoulders against the biting wind. "You just about did. Your dad got home a few minutes ago."

He sighed. "I stayed later to work on a group project. Idiotic crap. Anyway, you want to stay and eat with us?"

I shook my head. "I can't tonight, Jesse. I'm so behind on everything, and I promised Ava I'd be home to eat dinner with her. I'm sorry."

"That's okay." He tucked a strand of hair behind my ear and glanced at the kitchen window behind us. "C'mere."

He tugged my arm, pulling me until we were out of view, and then he wrapped me in his arms, his mouth on my lips.

I came up for air, gasping. "Was that persuasion?"

He laughed. "No, that was I'm-going-to-miss-you-but-I-understand." He tucked me a little tighter into his arms. "But did it persuade you to do anything?"

"Nope, sorry." I wriggled away. "Gotta run. Maybe see you Wednesday?"

"As far as I know. Matter of fact, why don't we make it a date? Plan on us going out to dinner after you're finished with the rug rat."

"That I can do. Talk to you tomorrow?"

"Definitely."

I did talk to Jesse on Tuesday, but not for very long. Submissions to the blog were flooding in now, and Kristen and I were swamped, going through emails and messages. Between that and my other school work, not to mention my new mission to plan a birthday party for my roommate, I hardly had time to breathe.

I sent out email invitations to the list of friends Ava had given me, and I posted a flyer about the party on our dorm community bulletin board. I assigned jobs to the freshman I considered most trustworthy, making sure to keep the crucial elements for myself. I even called Giff to make sure he knew that he was invited.

"Aren't you a brave little toaster, planning another birthday shindig? I hope this one lasts longer. And ends better."

"You and me both, buddy. Let me tell you, if it weren't Ava, I wouldn't be doing it. But she's been a little down lately. Something's bothering her. I thought a party might cheer her up."

I let that slip on purpose, hoping to find out if Giff knew anything about what had gone on between our respective roommates. But if he did, he didn't tell me.

"Well, I'll be there. And let me know if you need me to do anything meantime."

"I will. Oh, and Giff, not that you would, but please don't mention this party to Liam. The last thing I need is for him to show up at another party I'm throwing. Can you just imagine?"

"Gotcha. These lips are sealed. See you next week."

I was already frazzled by the time I got to work on Wednesday. Sarah met me at the door, not looking so great herself, and holding a sniffling little boy.

"He's got a cold, and he was up all night, miserable," she told me as I came inside. "I was going to call and tell you not to come today, but then I thought maybe...you might sit with him just for an hour. I need a little bit of sleep. Would you mind?"

"Of course not." I took Des from her. "Come on, sweet boy. We'll go read books, okay?"

He rubbed his eyes. "Watch Thomas?"

"Sure, let's go watch some choo-choos."

Sarah yawned. "Jules, you'll never know how much I appreciate this. Just to get an hour's nap..."

"Shoo. Go. We're good here. Anything I need to know about our little sickie here?"

She shook her head. "No, I just gave him some medicine, so he's good for another four hours. He has juice in his cup, and he can have some chicken noodle soup if he wants it—there's a pot in the fridge. Otherwise, just keep him happy. I'll be back down in a little bit." She shuffled down the hall and up the stairs.

Des and I watched train videos for about forty minutes before he fell asleep, leaning against my side and breathing heavily. I laid my head against the back of the sofa and closed my eyes, hoping that whatever germs were inhabiting the little guy didn't make the jump to me.

Danny came home before Sarah woke up. He tip-toed

into the living room on stocking feet, nodding when I put my finger to my lips.

"Poor baby." He whispered the words, shaking his head. "I came home early to give Sarah a break. Thanks for sticking around, Julia."

"No problem." I carefully disengaged myself from the sleeping baby. "Sarah's still asleep. And you don't look like you got much rest either."

"No, but more than Sarah."

All I wanted to do was get out of there, but Danny looked so pitiful that I heard myself saying, "If you sit down with Des, I'll make dinner. That way Sarah can sleep some more, and you can rest, too."

Danny sighed. "Thanks, Julia. What would we do without you?"

By the time I finished making spaghetti and meatballs, Des was awake. Sarah came downstairs, blinking in confusion as I was settling her son in the high chair. Jesse came in at the same time.

"What's going on?" He looked from his father to his little brother, frowning.

"The baby's sick, and Julia saved the day," Danny answered, patting my shoulder. "Take her out of here, Jess, before we decide to keep her for the night."

"Okay." Jesse glanced at me. "You all right?"

"Yeah. Let me just grab my bag and coat."

I scooped up everything as fast as I could and followed Jesse out the door, blowing kisses to Desmond as he slurped up his noodles.

"Thank you." I smiled up at Jesse, taking his hand as we headed toward the guest house. "They were so pitiful, I really was thinking I'd be there all night."

"Yeah, I didn't know Des was sick." Jesse unlocked the door and leaned to turn on a light, then stood back to let me go inside.

"I think it's just a cold. I'm crossing my fingers he didn't share it with me." I leaned against the edge of the sofa as Jesse went into the kitchen and opened the refrigerator. "So, do you still want to go out, or did you want me to make something here?"

Jesse turned around, and for the first time, I got a good look at his face. His eyes were distant and his mouth tight.

"Whatever works. I don't mind going out. You shouldn't have to cook after taking care of a sick kid all afternoon."

I stepped into the kitchen, feeling just a little off-kilter. I realized that Jesse hadn't made any move to touch me, aside from when I took his hand to walk over here.

"Jesse, is everything okay? If you don't want to go out tonight, we don't need to. I can just go back to campus."

"No, I'm--" He stopped and shook his head. "No, I'm not okay. I shouldn't say anything tonight, when you're so tired. But I need to know."

My heart sped up just a bit, and I licked my lips. "What do you need to know?"

"I had class today with Cal. Remember, you met him Sunday?"

I nodded, a wave of dread falling over me.

"Cal asked me how long we'd been dating. He said he knew the guy you used to date."

"That's not a secret, Jesse. I told you about Liam."

"Right, and I said that. But then he said..." Jesse drew a

deep breath. "He said since you broke up with Liam, you've been, um, seeing a lot of different guys. He said he's heard stuff about you."

I closed my eyes. "Jesse, it's not what you think."

His voice was low. "Then tell me what it is. I asked you the first time we went out if you were seeing anyone else. And you told me your ex was the only other person you've dated."

"And that's the truth. I'm not seeing anyone but you. I haven't. Jesse, it's complicated. It just wasn't the right time to explain everything to you then. It would have seemed weird."

"What would have? You're talking in circles. And why wouldn't you just tell me whatever it is that's so complicated?"

"Because things have changed since we started dating. It doesn't matter anymore."

Jesse leaned his back against the fridge. "It matters to me."

"Okay. Do you mind if I sit down?"

He spread his hand in a be-my-guest gesture. I sank into the same easy chair where we'd sat together during the Super Bowl.

"I told you my break up with Liam was messy. I'm going to assume you haven't heard exactly what happened."

Jesse shrugged. "Cal said something about a birthday party."

"Yeah, it was Liam's birthday party. The surprise party I threw him. He showed up, late, drunk and with his hands on the tits of another girl."

Jesse's eyes flickered. "Shit."

"Yeah. On top of that, because he hadn't embarrassed me enough, he announced right there that he had broken up with me. Apparently, he had just neglected to tell me about it."

Jesse nodded. "I'm sorry. That's must have sucked."

"Just a little. We'd been dating for over ten months. He did it on purpose. I was..." I cast my eyes up. "Oh, I don't know. I wasn't heartbroken, but I was mad. And hurt. And humiliated."

"And that's why you started going out with lots of guys?"

"No. Well, not really." He was going to make me say it out loud. "I came back from Christmas break, and I still couldn't stop thinking about how mad I was at Liam. So Ava and I came up with an idea. I know it sounds immature or crazy. And even saying it now makes me feel stupid. But I decided I needed revenge. So we came up with this idea to get back at Liam by making him want me back. Our friend Giff—well, he's Liam's roommate, but he thought Liam and I should get back together—and he set me up with all these guys, to make Liam think I was dating them. So that's why I was doing it."

Jesse frowned, nodding slowly. "I guess I see. All the guys Cal was talking about—they were all set ups?"

"Yes. I know it sounds idiotic. All I can say is at the time, it made some kind of sense. But nothing happened with any of them, other than being out where Liam might see us. And after we started dating, I told Giff I was out. I haven't seen anyone else but you since then. I promise."

"So you've given up on the revenge plans against Liam?"

I fiddled with the button on my coat. "Yes. Well...mostly. I was going to use the blog I'm doing to write about what Liam did to me. That's what gave me the idea for the whole thing. But I changed my mind, and I'm not doing it now."

Jesse came around the counter and sat down on the sofa. He kept his eyes on the floor in front of us.

"Is that all of it?"

I took a deep breath. "For me, yes. But then Liam started messing with Ava. He kissed her, tried to get her to see him. Go out with him. If I hadn't told her what he said to me after the wrestling match, it might still be going on."

"What did he say to you after the wrestling match? What wrestling match?"

I swallowed. "I told you about that. Kind of. Remember I said I had run into my ex and he had said some crap to me? He offered me the fabulous opportunity to be his booty call babe. He said he'd be willing to sleep with me without strings. So I didn't have to keep seeing all those other guys."

Jesse shook his head. "Yeah, he's an asshole."

I leaned forward. "So you see why I wanted to get back at him? To teach him a lesson?"

"I guess I can. To a point. But Julia, once we started going out, didn't it change things?"

I nodded and got up to sit next to him on the sofa. "Of course it did. After I met you, I didn't care about getting back at Liam. I realized anything I did wasn't going to change him, and I didn't care, anyway. Ava's birthday party was her idea."

"What does Ava's birthday party have to do with any of it?"

I realized I hadn't explained that. "I'm throwing the party for her. I told you he's been trying to get her to go out with him. She's inviting Liam, and when he gets there, she's going to turn him down, once and for all. Tell everyone he's been after her, and then...humiliate him. Publicly. In front of all our friends."

Jesse dropped his head into his hands. "Julia, I can't do this. I don't like games. I've been honest with you since we met, and now I'm not even sure I know you."

Tears choked me. "Jesse, you do. I haven't been dishonest. I was just—I don't know, a little crazy for a while. Liam made me miserable, but when I met you, I realized how much I'd been missing. I promise you, who I am with you is the real me. The only me. For good or for bad. And I'm sorry I didn't tell you sooner. I knew it was in my past, and I hoped it wouldn't matter."

He leaned back on the sofa, staring at the ceiling. "Remember how I asked you the first night we went out if I were your rebound guy? That's important to me. My mom and dad got together after my dad broke up with the girl he thought was the love of his life. He tried with my mom, he really did, but she always knew she was second best. Or at least she felt that way. It's what caused their divorce. I never want to be someone's second choice."

I ventured out a fingertip to touch his hand. "You are not my second choice, Jesse. You're my only choice. I wasn't lying when I said Liam didn't mean anything to me."

Jesse rubbed his forehead. "I need to think, Julia. I need some time. And you need to make some decisions, too. I don't want to be part of any payback plans. Not even for Ava."

I nodded. "I understand." I stood and picked up my bag. "I'll go now. Just--" Tears filled my eyes and ran down my face, and I fled before Jesse could see them. Flinging open the door, I stumbled blindly toward my car, my hand shaking as I pulled out the keys.

"Julia." Jesse stood in the doorway, anguish in his voice. "Don't. You're upset, you shouldn't drive."

I finally found the right key and opened the door. I couldn't speak, couldn't answer him. I threw my bag into the car and wiped at my eyes just enough to clear my vision. Mindful of Danny and Sarah, I pulled out slowly, until I got to the end of the driveway and turned onto the road.

Then I floored it and drove home as fast as I could.

Chapter Twenty

If I thought Liam's betrayal had crushed me, I was sadly mistaken. Losing him after ten months of dating didn't even begin to touch how I felt knowing I'd hurt Jesse.

Jesse texted me that night to make sure I got home. When I didn't answer, he called, over and over, until finally I sent him a one-word response.

Since then, I'd heard nothing.

Ava was beside herself. "It's my fault. I never should have come up with that plan. And I'm sorry, about the idea for the birthday party, Jules. Call it off. I'm not going through with it."

I sniffed, swallowing back more tears. "We're not canceling your party, Ave. As far as what happens with Liam, that's up to you. I'm done with it. With him."

"But Jesse..." Her voice trailed, but there was worry in

her eyes.

I held down a sob. "I screwed up everything with Jesse, and it's not your fault. You told me all along, that I should stop and think about it. God, Ava, what was I doing? I'm not in high school. I'm supposed to be smarter than this. And all I've done is mess up the one good thing in my life."

I dragged through the next week, sleeping through classes and walking campus like a zombie. I dreaded going back to work on Friday, but I didn't have to worry; Sarah called and told me that though Desmond was getting over his cold, he was still fussy and she had decided to stay home with him.

Part of me wondered if Jesse had said something to her about us, but then she added, "I hope you don't come down with it. Jesse will not be happy with me if you do."

I laughed awkwardly and told her I'd see her the next week. But even though Danny got home a little later both days, I didn't see Jesse on Monday or Wednesday.

Kristen came over on Thursday after seminar so that we could work on the final posts for the blog.

"Are you okay?" She eyed me critically. "No offense, but you look like hell."

I tried a smile. "I've been better. I don't want to talk about it, if it's okay with you."

"Sure, no problem. So do we want to finish up with your story as our big finale?" We'd run a slightly altered version of Kristen's heartbreak the week before. Response had been huge; it had generated so much discussion, we'd run a second, follow-up post a few days later.

"No." I shook my head. "I don't want to put mine in. I'm sorry, Kristen. I'm not wimping out, I just don't want to hurt anyone. The details are too specific." I paused. "But I'd like to write the round-up if you don't mind. I think I have something to say."

"Fine with me. What are you going to write?"

"Just what we've learned. That it's both sexes experiencing bad break-ups and cheating. That there are usually two sides to any story. And that the best revenge is moving on."

Kristen nodded. "I like it. I think we're going to get an A on this."

She stood, stretching. "Thanks for letting me do this assignment with you, Julia. It was very..." She glanced past me. "Healing."

"I'm glad. Just don't tell Dr. Turner it gave you closure."

Kristen raised her eyebrows. "Okay. I'll see you in class next week."

After she left, I curled up in bed, pulling the comforter to my chin. Ava had gone home for the night to have an early celebration of her birthday with her family. She rarely went away anywhere, and it was odd for me to have the room to myself overnight. But I wasn't going to complain. A night to just lay around and wallow in my misery was about all I was up to doing at this point.

My eyes drifted shut. I hadn't been sleeping well the last few nights, and I began to doze.

"You know I can't resist you all warm and sleepy."

Still disoriented, I struggled to sit up straight in bed. Jesse stood in the doorway of my room, his eyes steady on me.

I laid a hand over my chest. "You scared the hell out of me."

"Sorry. The door wasn't quite latched. When I went to knock, it opened."

I nodded. "Kristen just left. She must not have closed it on her way out."

Jesse leaned against the door jam, hands in the pockets of his jacket. "Can I come in?" He glanced down the hallway. "I'd rather talk without the audience."

"Oh, yeah, come in. You can shut the door." I tried to smooth my hair down.

Jesse sat down on the end of the bed, looking nearly as nervous as I felt. I saw his chest rise as he took a deep breath.

"Julia, I'm sorry about the other night. I was upset. Cal said some pretty nasty things, and I told him he didn't know what he was talking about. I was pissed. I wanted you to tell me it was ridiculous, that Cal was lying."

I closed my eyes. "I'm sorry."

"No. You told me the truth. And I see why you didn't say anything before. At least, once I thought about it, I understood."

I lifted one shoulder. "I wanted to. At first I thought it was too soon, and then it didn't seem to matter." I ventured a glance at his face. "But it's all over. It's done. I'm not even putting the story on our blog. Jesse, Liam doesn't mean anything to me. You're not my rebound boyfriend."

"I know." He slid closer and framed my face in his hands. "I'm sorry I said that. I've put up with all the crap my parents put Ali and me through. I never want to end up where they are. But I jumped to crazy conclusions." He leaned his forehead against mine, while his thumbs feathered my cheeks. "I've been a mess the last few days. I missed you."

I tried to blink back the tears. "I missed you, too. I

234

thought I screwed everything up for us."

"Nah. This is just a bump in the road." His mouth touched mine. "Clean slate, right?"

I managed a smile. "Clean slate. No more revenge. No more secrets. Only you and me."

"You and me. I like that." He kissed me with the same intensity that made me want to pull him into bed with me—and never come back out.

"Jesse?" I spoke against his lips.

"IImmm?"

"Ava's away all night. I have the room to myself."

He leaned back, eyebrows raised as he looked down at me and then glanced over my shoulder, out the window, where dark was just beginning to take over.

"It *is* late." He ran a hand around to the back of my neck.

"Probably too late for you to drive home," I agreed, ignoring the clock on my desk that read 6:50 PM.

"My first class tomorrow isn't until eleven. Plenty of time to go back home in the daylight."

"You'd be doing me a favor. Keeping me from being lonely and afraid."

He sighed. "You know me, Julia...selfless to a fault." He shifted so that I fell back to my pillow, and he covered my body with his, stifling any smart comeback I might have had by kissing me into submission.

"Lacey, where are the paper plates?" I stood in the middle of the lounge. All around me, freshman girls were taping up crepe paper and inflating balloons, chattering and giggling so that I could hardly think.

"I gave them to Patty." The blonde girl blinked at me. "She said she was in charge of paper products."

"Okay. Go get Stephanie and make sure the plates and plastic ware are put on the table in the front." I turned around, checking my mental list of last minute things to do.

"Jules, where do want all this ice?" Jesse carried in the cooler. Through his thin cotton shirt, the muscles in his arms stood out, and I felt the sigh that rippled through the girls around us.

"By the drink tub, please. Thanks." I watched him carrying the ice across the room.

"Julia, the music's all set. And Becca said to tell you the last of the food is coming up now."

"Perfect."

"Everything looks so pretty." Ava came in, smiling. "Jules, thank you so much." She laid a hand on Jesse's arm. "I'm glad you're here. It's going to be fun tonight."

"I hope so. As long as you're happy, so am I. You deserve a kick-ass party."

"And that's just what this is going to be." Jesse laced his fingers through mine and squeezed my hand as more people began to arrive.

"Jules! Everything looks perfect." Giff hugged me hard. "You're getting to be a pro. Parties by Julia. Nah, that's too plain. I'll have to come up with something better."

"Yeah, no thanks. I think I'll keep my day job." I grinned up at him, glad he had come. "At least no one's going to be surprised at this one. I hope." I tightened my fingers within Jesse's and tugged him forward. "Jesse, this is my friend, Giff. Giff, this is Jesse Fleming. My boyfriend."

Giff's eyes missed nothing, taking in our linked hands. He smiled.

"Good to meet you, Jesse. I hope you're taking good care of our girl here. She deserves it. She's a keeper."

Jesse pulled me in front of him, wrapping his arms around my waist. "I happen to agree. And don't worry, I'm doing my best to keep her in line."

"Julia, we can't find the napkins!" I rolled my eyes as a panicked freshman clutched my arm.

"Excuse me, guys. I need to go avert a crisis."

By the time I got back to the lounge, the room was full and loud. I smiled at a few people as I made my way back to Jesse, who was talking with Giff and some other boys I didn't recognize. Ava stood to the side, chatting with her fellow psych majors. She was so pretty in her short black dress. It made her skin look even more translucent and picked up the shine of her hair. For the first time in weeks, she looked relaxed, too, and I was glad that I'd gone along with the idea for the party. Even if our goal had changed, we were celebrating my best friend.

Just as I reached Jesse's side, the atmosphere in the room changed abruptly. The noise level in the room dropped to almost nothing. When I saw Giff's face, tight and angry, looking at something over my shoulder, I already knew what had happened.

Liam stood just within the doorway.

It was like a weird flash of de-je vu, except this time, Liam was by himself. There was no girl hanging onto him. He was dressed in a long-sleeved button up shirt and dark jeans, and his eyes skimmed the crowd. His gaze paused only for a fraction of a moment as it passed over me, then moved on and fastened on Ava.

She had turned at the same time I did, and their eyes met. Something I didn't understand flashed between them, and then Ava stepped backward, her bottom lip trembling.

Jesse closed a hand around my shoulder. "Is that him?" he murmured low into my ear. "Do you want me to throw him out?"

I was tempted for just a moment. It would have been sweet. And then I thought of Ava. The last thing I wanted to do was to ruin her beautiful party. As Dr. Turner had said, this wasn't about closure. It was about moving on.

Without a second thought, I stepped through the crowd again, this time walking toward Liam. He saw me, and trepidation flashed in his eyes. People stood aside as I went past, but no one moved too far: nobody wanted to miss the show.

I stood for a beat in front of him, and then I held out my hand.

"So glad you could make it, Liam. Come on, get something to eat." I glanced back behind me. "Ava's over there. I know you want to tell her happy birthday." I raised my voice just a bit, smiling. "Eat up, everyone! I'm bringing out the cake in about half an hour."

There was a surge toward the food table, and I let out a quiet breath of relief. Jesse found me and pulled me into his arms.

"That was amazing." He kissed the side of my neck and then leaned back, looking down at me. "Did you know you're pretty much perfect?"

I laughed, still a little shaky, and leaned into him, glad

to have the solid promise of his chest beneath my cheek. "Not hardly. But believe it or not, that felt better than any payback I'd imagined." I raised my head to touch my lips to Jesse's chin. "Mostly because of you."

The rest of the party went exactly as planned, to my enormous relief. There was no more drama, no more surprise guests. We brought out the cake ablaze with candles, everyone sang happy birthday, and then Ava cut it forever, it seemed, handing out slices on the pretty paper plates. After that, the crowd began to thin out, as people left for other parties or dates. I stood with Jesse, just watching. He was leaning against the wall, and I leaned against him, running my hands over his forearms as they rested on my stomach.

"I love your arms." I trailed my fingernails lightly from his hands to his elbows. "Is that weird?"

He nuzzled my neck. "Not at all. Whatever part of my body turns you on, I'm just happy it does."

I craned my neck to meet his eyes. "All of you turns me on." I wiggled a little against him and was rewarded when he sucked in a quick breath.

"Julia." Liam stood in front of us, holding a red plastic cup as though it were his lifeline.

"Hi, Liam." I rested my head back on Jesse's chest. "Have you met Jesse yet?"

"No." He nodded in Jesse's direction. "Liam Bailey."

"Yeah." Jesse didn't move except to tighten his grip on me. "I know."

"So I take you two are...together?"

I smiled. I couldn't help it. "Yes, we are."

"Good." Liam looked from one of us to the other. "Julia's a terrific girl. I hope you guys are happy. Take care of her." He shifted his gaze to me. "I'm sure you deserve her more than I did."

"I'm pretty sure, too." Jesse's voice was hard. "And I don't plan on letting her go. I know a good thing when I've got it."

Liam winced just a little. "Julia, thank you for tonight. You were better to me than I could have expected. Considering how the last party went down, I mean."

I nodded. "Water under the bridge, Liam. I've gotten over it. I hope you can, too."

"Maybe I will." His eyes skittered away and fastened on Ava, who was sitting in the corner, eating a piece of cake with Giff.

"Liam." I caught his attention again. "Don't mess with her. She's not like you. She doesn't play games."

He shrugged. "I'm not playing anything." He looked away again and then smiled at us. "Good to meet you, Jesse. Julia, thanks again. Great party." He turned, and I knew he was heading toward Ava and Gifford.

"Hey." Jesse caught my chin, turned it toward his face. "Ava's a big girl. She can take care of herself."

I nodded. "I guess so. I just worry." I swiveled so that I was flush against Jesse's body, pressing him into the wall. "If Ava doesn't need me, who will I take care of now?"

A slow smile spread across his face. "I can think of someone."

Chapter Twenty-One

"That was an amazing meal." Jesse leaned back from the table. "Steak and potatoes. That's man's food."

I rolled my eyes. "Okay, caveman. Guess what? Dishes are waiting for you. You know the rules. I cooked, you wash."

"Hey, I made the steak."

"Um, no. I bought the steak, marinated it, seasoned it. You borrowed your dad's grill and cooked it. Matter of fact, if I wasn't keeping my eye on the timer, you would have burned it."

"Not my fault the Phillies went into extra innings. I had to keep running back and forth from the grill to the TV."

"Whatever. My point is that I did most of the cooking. So man up and do those dishes."

Jesse gave an exaggerated sigh as he went to the sink. I

carried our plates to him.

"I'm just glad it's warm enough to grill now." I covered the bowl of potatoes and put them into the fridge. "It's been a beautiful spring."

"True." Jesse squirted dish liquid into the sink. "Beach weather pretty soon."

"Hmm. I can't wait." I wrapped my arms around his waist and lay my cheek against his back. There was just something about a man doing dishes...

I moved my hands over his flat stomach, feeling his muscles bunch and tense. Want and need combined to pool low in my belly, and I rubbed against his back, relishing the sensation of his hard body on my breasts.

"Watch it there, woman." Jesse's voice was rough. "Keep that up, and these dishes will have to soak."

I smiled and let my hands sag lower, to the button of the cotton shorts he wore. He sucked in his breath, then let it out in a rush as I walked my fingers even lower, to the hard ridge beneath his fly. His hands stilled in the water.

"Jesse." I spoke softly into his back. "I don't want to wait anymore."

He paused a beat before answering me. "You mean...for me to finish the dishes?"

"I mean, for anything. I don't want to wait anymore. I want, now."

In a flurry of movement that made me gasp, he turned, and I was leaning into his chest, his arms wrapped around me. I shivered at the feel of his wet hands through my t-shirt.

"Are you sure?" He whispered the words, but I heard them clearly. I pulled his head so that I could take his mouth against mine, open as I dipped my tongue within.

"Really sure."

Jesse didn't need to hear anymore, clearly. He lifted me up, stopped only long enough to make sure the front door was locked, and carried me to the bedroom.

He laid me on the bed with great care. I had come to know these past months how gentle and soft his touch was, and he reminded me of that now. He peeled off his own shirt and then sat next to me on the bed, tugging at the hem of my tee.

He took care not to pull my hair or catch the shirt on my earrings as he took it off over my head. And then he lay down alongside me. His hands moved surely over my body, by now more familiar with what brought me pleasure.

He kissed me, with the same intensity I loved, and then he licked down my neck, teasing with his tongue. His fingers were already fondling my breasts, and when his mouth reached that spot, he laved one nipple through the cup of my bra while he rolled the other between his fingers, sending a jolt straight through me.

"Jesse!" I gasped.

"Hmmm?" He unhooked my bra and re-captured a nipple. "What?"

"Feels so good." I moaned the words and felt his smile as he circled his tongue around one peak.

"Mmm, I know. I love your breasts." He palmed them, bringing the other nipple to his mouth.

Even as his mouth continue to lick and nip, his hands moved between my legs. He disposed of my shorts easily, tugging them down my legs and then pulling my underwear off as well.

I ran my hands over his chest as he came back to lie next

to me. "No fair. You still have clothes on."

"I guess someone should take care of that." He grinned.

Reaching to his shorts, I unbuttoned and unzipped, then used my feet to move them down his legs. I reached for him through his boxers and was rewarded with the hiss of his breath as I gripped his length.

"God, Jules." He fell back on the bed, and I took advantage, leaning up on my elbow over him.

"Smile," I commanded, and used to my request by now, he did. As soon as his dimples appeared, I covered each one with my mouth, running my tongue over it with sensual abandon. I dropped kisses along his jaw to his chest, laying half on top of him as I took him in my hand again.

We'd become more adventurous over our months together. I touched Jesse as much as he did me, but we'd never crossed that last boundary. I felt him grow even harder as I moved my hand up and down.

"Jules." He flipped me over and fastened his mouth on my breast again. "I want to make you feel good first."

His fingers searched between my legs, finding the one spot that me arch and gasp. He rubbed slowly at first, with increasing pressure as I moaned louder, tensing. Just as I teetered on the edge, he stopped, kneeling up and away from me for a moment to fumble in the drawer of his nightstand. I heard the ripping of paper and opened my eyes to watch him roll on the condom.

He lay back down next to me, bringing his fingers to the heat at my center once again.

"Julia." I opened my eyes to find his face close to mine. "I wanted to say this before. I didn't want you to think it was just because of what we're doing. I love you. If you didn't know that—I do."

I smiled against his lips as they touched mine. "I love you, too, Jesse."

He moved his fingers faster over the nerves that made me insane. And just when I thought I would explode or die, he raised himself between my legs.

"You're sure?" He asked the question one last time, although I could see the strain of holding back in his face.

"I'm sure. Oh, God, Jesse, please!"

He didn't wait another minute. He sank into me on a long sigh, and I reared up to meet him, every inch of my skin hyper-aware of his body touching me. He linked his hands with mine, pressing them into the bed as he rose over me, pulling out with incredible slowness and then stroking within as he moved deeper.

I closed my eyes and fell into the pleasure. There was no one on my mind, in my heart, beyond Jesse. Every time he touched me, I felt his strength, how much he cared for me. When he lowered his mouth to brush over my lips, tenderly, almost reverently, my breath caught.

"Jules." He rocked into me again, and I wasn't sure why I wasn't exploding into a million pieces. "This—you-are everything I ever wanted."

Beyond words, wrapped only in his touch, I half-moaned, half-sighed a response. Jesse raised our joined hands above my head, and I opened my eyes to look up at him. He smiled, then buried himself deep into me. The most intense, incredible pleasure overcame me, and I'm pretty sure I screamed his name. At least once.

He continued to move, steady and sure, until the spasms from the aftermath of my own pleasure tightened around him. Then with one last thrust, he growled, every muscle in his body tightening as he found release.

I couldn't breathe for several seconds. My heart was racing, and every nerve in my body was ultra sensitive, alive.

Jesse collapsed onto the bed next to me, drawing me into his body and stroking back my hair.

"That," he murmured, "was worth waiting for. I love you, Julia."

I lay my head against his chest and listened to the thundering of his heart. "I love you, Jesse."

Outside, the day ended and the sun set. Within that room, lying in his arms, I had everything I had ever wanted.

Epilogue

"Ava, please. I just want to talk."

Ava closed her eyes. "Liam, no. Please. Go away." She wished he hadn't let him into her room. Julia was with Jesse for the weekend, and that meant no one would be coming in to rescue her. She rubbed her hands across her forehead.

"You can't tell me you don't feel anything for me. God, Ava, when I kiss you...it's like everything in the world disappears. I don't want to stop. Ever."

"Well, you have to!" Ava tried to keep her voice down; freshman girls were curious, and she was sure more than one had noticed that Liam Bailey was visiting her room with alarming regularity.

"Why?" He moved closer, reaching to touch her, but Ava ducked away. His touch was not a good idea. It robbed her of the ability to think clearly.

"Because, Liam, this is wrong. You don't care for me. You've talked yourself into thinking you do, for some reason I just don't understand. But you don't know me, and I'm not picking up for you where Julia left off. You forget, I saw firsthand how miserable you made her. No, thanks. I'm not signing up for that tour."

He sighed. "It's not the same. Julia and I were a mistake. But Ava, I have never felt about anyone the way I feel about you. Just give me a chance to prove it."

Ava felt like screaming. That voice in her head that kept telling her to take a chance, to let him in, was getting stronger. Pretty soon it would drown out the other voice, the sensible one that reminded her that Liam Bailey was a jerk, and she would give in again, let him kiss her, touch her...

"No." She said it out loud to strengthen her resolve. "Not again. Not this time." She tightened her jaw and swallowed. It was time to play her last card, to get rid of Liam once and for all.

"Liam, you think you really like me, don't you?" Ava forced lightness into her voice. "You think it's different with us, right?"

"Yes." He spoke with relief, thinking that she was hearing him at last.

"Good." Ava clenched her fists. "I'm glad. Because now I can tell you..." She took a deep breath and plunged in. "I don't feel anything for you. Nothing but...pity." She let that sink in. "After what you did to my best friend, did you seriously think I could even look at you? I've been playing you, Liam. Just waiting for this moment. You know what they say about revenge, right? Well, it's been worth the wait."

She finally raised her eyes to his face. Pain and something else warred behind his eyes, and she had to steel herself not to cross the room to hold him, to reach up and kiss away the hurt.

"That's it?" His words were clipped. "This was all a way to get back at me? You expect me to believe that?"

"Believe it or not. It's the truth." She bit the side of her mouth hard, holding back the sobs that were gathering in her chest. She had to be strong for just a few more minutes, just until he left the room.

"I thought...I thought this was different. *We* were different. But the whole time, this was just a game to you."

Ava couldn't speak anymore. She nodded.

Liam turned. He paused for a minute in the doorway of the room, and for a crazy beat of her heart, Ava prayed he would come back in, see her for the liar she was.

But he didn't. He kept walking, away from her, out of her life.

When she knew she could move again without running after him, Ava walked across the room, closed the door behind him and locked it. Then she climbed into her bed, curled up on her side, and cried into her pillow, deep, silent sobs wracking her body until the whole bed shook.

She lay there for hours, until the tears were gone and only numbness was left.

Revenge was not sweet. It felt like death, and it hurt worse than anything Ava had ever known.

Coming Soon

Just Desserts

Ava's Story

Acknowledgements

I'm a long-winded acknowledger, always, because I couldn't do half of what I do without the support and help of so many.

First, because he figures so much in this book, my eternal thanks and gratitude to Joss Whedon. Because you are a freaking genius and you leave me breathless with your talent.

Thanks to my Hayson and Promotional Book Tours family, who make me laugh, who jump into the fray without question, who are always there to share, to post and to promote. You all rock my world daily.

To Stephanie Nelson of Once Upon a Time book covers, for this amazing, gorgeous cover. Thank you for your patience and talent! Get the guest room ready, I am so coming for a visit.

To Stacey Blake for her daily, hourly, minutely help and support, and especially for her beautiful formatting. You take a good story and make it look pretty!

Mandie. . .there are never enough words for your love and encouragement. I am blessed to be on this adventure with you!

Amanda Latzel Long, I owe you a humongous debt of gratitude for your help and input on this book. From cover ideas to beta reading and proofing. . .your help was indispensable. How many people can you ask, "How was the sex?" without sounding insecure? Thank you so much for everything you do. . .when I get you back down to Florida, there's a bottle of wine and trip to H&M in your future. At least.

To my family, who has now become used to Mommy's craziness as I get deep into a book, thank you for you love, your patience and everything you do to make my life possible and infinitely more fun. I love you so much.

And finally to my readers, who have cheered me along through each new book, left reviews and shared posts. . .you rock, and you make my job my joy.

About the Author

Photo: Marilyn Bellinger

Tawdra Thompson Kandle lives in central Florida with her husband, children, cats and dog. She loves homeschooling, cooking, traveling and reading, not necessarily in that order. And yes, she has purple hair.

You can follow Tawdra here...

Facebook:https://www.facebook.com/AuthorTawdraKandle

Twitter:https://twitter.com/tawdra

Website: tawdrakandle.com

Other Books from Hayson Publishing

Through the Valley Love Endures by Eddie David
Santiago

All for Hope by Olivia Hardin

The King Series by Tawdra Kandle
Fearless
Breathless
Restless
Endless

The Posse by Tawdra Kandle

Imperfection by Phaedra Seabolt

Annie Crow Knoll: Sunrise by Gail Priest

Tough Love by Marcie A. Bridges

Haunted U by Jessica Gibson